Cowboy's Redemption

Nicole Simon

Published by Nicole Simon, 2024.

COWBOY'S REDEMPTION

First edition. February 2, 2024.

Copyright © 2024 Nicole Simon.

ISBN: 979-8224394890

Written by Nicole Simon.

Cowboy's Redemption

A Western Romance Mystery

By Nicole Simon

© Copyright 2024 - All rights reserved.

Chapter 1: The Disappearance

The wind moaned as it whipped through the barren branches that clawed at the sky, casting eerie shadows on the ground. A raven cawed ominously from its perch, bearing dark tidings. The melancholy atmosphere hung heavy over the small town, reflecting the turmoil that plagued the hearts of its inhabitants. Amelia Montgomery, the beloved daughter of the owners of Montgomery Ranch, had vanished without a trace.

Jackson Turner had just come to visit his mother, Margaret, who met him at the door with a worried expression. "Jackson, dear, I think you should take this call. It's the second time today that they've called here looking for you."

"Who is it?" Jackson asked, wiping the sweat from his brow and untangling his fingers from the reins of his horse. He tethered the animal outside and stepped into the warm embrace of the modest house.

"It's Mr. Montgomery," Margaret replied, her voice hushed and urgent. She handed him the telephone receiver, her hands trembling ever so slightly.

"Mr. Montgomery? It's been a while since I've seen him," said Jackson, confusion settling in alongside the exhaustion that weighed upon him. His mind raced, struggling to find any reason for such an abrupt call.

"Jackson, is that you?" The rich baritone of Amelia's father boomed through the telephone line, filling the room with an urgency that ignited a spark of concern in Jackson's chest.

"Yes, sir, it's me," Jackson stammered, gripping the receiver tighter. "What can I do for you?"

"Amelia's missing, Jackson. She's been gone for two days now, and we don't have a single lead. You know how close you two were growing up... We've always admired your wit and resourcefulness. You're the only person I can trust to get to the bottom of this. Please, son, I'm begging you – help me find my daughter."

As the words tumbled out of Mr. Montgomery's mouth, the desperation in his voice struck a chord deep within Jackson's soul. Amelia had been more than just a childhood friend. He'd had a crush on her for years and considered her the embodiment of all that was good and pure in the dusty plains they called home.

"Of course," Jackson answered without hesitation. "I'll do everything in my power to find her. I promise."

The moment the call ended, Jackson's mind churned like a steam engine racing down the tracks. He couldn't shake the image of Amelia, her beautiful auburn hair dancing in the wind as they played together on those endless sun-soaked days. He clenched his fists and gritted his teeth, determined not to let his friend vanish without a trace.

"Amelia, I swear I'll find you," he muttered under his breath, his voice a mix of anger and steadfast resolution.

With haste, Jackson gathered his essentials – his trusty revolver, ammunition, and worn leather cowboy hat – then saddled up his loyal mare, Butterscotch. The sun was still low in the sky, casting long shadows across the arid landscape as they set off toward the Montgomery Ranch. He kept his thoughts locked on Amelia, replaying their memories together, fueling his resolve to bring her back safely.

As the terrain rolled beneath him, soft hues of orange and red painted the Montana sky, hinting at the vibrant world that awaited beyond the rugged expanse of the wild west. The air was thick with the scent of sagebrush and dust, carrying whispers of untold stories from the land that time had forgotten.

Finally, the grandiose entrance of the Montgomery Ranch came into view. Its wooden gates stood tall and proud, flanked by two stone pillars adorned with the family's emblem – an intricately carved M intertwined with a golden horseshoe.

As Jackson approached the entrance, the gates creaked open to reveal a stoic-faced man whose eyes held both gratitude and apprehension. "Jackson, thanks for coming," he said, extending a hand to help Jackson dismount. "We've been expecting you."

"Thank you," Jackson replied, nodding curtly as he accepted the assistance. His heart raced in anticipation while his keen eyes scanned the ranch, searching for any clue that might lead him to Amelia's whereabouts.

The opulence of the Montgomery Ranch was evident in every detail, but beneath this veneer of wealth and extravagance, an unsettling tension permeated the air, as if the very walls were holding their breath.

"Jackson," said a soft voice, pulling Jackson from his thoughts. A woman with auburn hair and eyes that mirrored Amelia's stood before him, her hands wringing nervously. "I'm so glad you've come."

"Mrs. Montgomery," Jackson replied, taking her offered hand gently. "I'll do everything in my power to find Amelia."

"Thank you," she whispered, tears welling in her eyes. "We're all at a loss. I just don't understand how she could vanish without a trace."

"Sometimes," Jackson began, his voice steady and reassuring, "it's the smallest details that can lead us to the truth." He paused, studying the worried faces of Amelia's family and friends gathered around them. It was clear they were placing their hope in him.

"Let's start by retracing Amelia's steps the day she disappeared," he suggested, meeting each gaze with determination. "I need to know everything she did, everywhere she went, and everyone she spoke to."

"Of course," Mrs. Montgomery replied, composing herself. "We'll tell you all we know."

"Okay," Jackson said, his mind racing with possibilities as they began to share their accounts of Amelia's last known movements. The rugged cowboy knew he would leave no stone unturned in his search for answers. Amelia's loved ones were counting on him, and he would not let them down.

"Amelia," Jackson thought, his heart heavy with the weight of responsibility, "you've always been like a sister to me. I won't rest until I find you." And with that promise etched into his mind, he embarked on his most important adventure yet – one that would challenge his skills, his resolve, and perhaps even his heart.

***

Jackson began his search in Amelia's bedroom, the morning sun casting a golden glow over the elegant furnishings. The opulence of the room couldn't mask the feeling of emptiness and despair that hung heavily in the air.

"Alright, Amelia," he muttered to himself, rolling up his sleeves. "Let's see what you've left for us." His keen eyes scanned the room, taking in every detail. He hoped that the key to finding her lay hidden somewhere within these walls.

He approached her ornate writing desk, noticing the scattered papers and an inkwell knocked askew. It appeared as though Amelia had been in a hurry – or perhaps something had startled her. A cryptic note caught his eye, hastily scribbled on a piece of torn parchment. The words seemed nonsensical at first glance: "Four horses, one heart, the river runs red."

"Interesting..." Jackson mused, furrowing his brow as he pocketed the note. He would need to decipher its meaning later, but every clue mattered in this investigation.

Next, he moved to her closet, carefully examining the contents. Amidst the neatly folded clothes, he found a torn photograph. It depicted Amelia with a group of friends, laughing and carefree. But someone had deliberately scratched out the face of one man in the picture. Jackson recognized the tattered remnants of the man's grin – it belonged to a local ranch hand named Thomas.

"Why did you scratch out Thomas's face, Amelia?" he whispered, as if expecting an answer from the silent room. This new piece of evidence added another layer to the mystery, and Jackson couldn't shake the feeling that it was significant.

"Amelia, what are you trying to tell us?" He asked the empty room, frustration building inside him. He knew that time was running out. With each passing moment, Amelia could be in more danger.

As he continued searching the room, he noticed a misplaced book on her nightstand. It was an old collection of Western love stories, well-worn from countless readings. And nestled between the pages, he discovered another clue – a dried wildflower, its once-vibrant petals now faded.

"Of all the flowers, you chose this one," Jackson said softly, his thoughts racing as he tried to piece together the puzzle Amelia had left behind. "What's your connection to this flower?"

With each new clue, Jackson's determination only grew stronger. He knew Amelia's family was counting on him to unravel the mystery surrounding her disappearance, and he refused to let them down.

***

The sun dipped below the horizon, casting a golden glow across the sprawling Montgomery Ranch. Jackson stood outside the stables, dust swirling around his boots as he prepared to interview the ranch hands. He knew that someone here might hold the key to Amelia's disappearance, and he was determined to unearth every possible lead.

"Evenin', Mr. Turner," greeted Hank, the burly stable manager, as he strode towards Jackson. "You got some questions for us?"

"Yes, I do," Jackson replied, tipping his hat in acknowledgement. "I'm tryin' to piece together Amelia's last known whereabouts, and I need all the help I can get."

As they walked through the stables, Jackson observed the ranch hands closely. Their furrowed brows and guarded expressions only added to the atmosphere of tension already hanging over the ranch. He started by asking them about Amelia's behavior and routines.

"Amelia loved her horse, Sundance," said one young ranch hand, his voice trembling slightly. "She'd always come down here to ride her, no matter how busy she was."

"Did you see anything unusual on the day she disappeared?" Jackson pressed, his keen eyes studying the man's face.

"Can't say I did," he replied, shifting uncomfortably under Jackson's gaze. "But, uh, there was that newcomer who arrived a few days before. A drifter, I think. Seemed a bit... off, if you ask me."

"Okay," Jackson mused, filing away the information for later consideration. "Do you know where I might find this drifter?"

"Last I saw, he was working over at the old Thompson place," the boy said hesitantly, as if unsure whether he should be sharing such knowledge.

"Thank you, son," Jackson replied, giving the young man a reassuring pat on the shoulder. "Your information could be very valuable."

As he moved from one witness to another, Jackson's thoughts churned with possibilities. Who was this drifter? Could he be involved in Amelia's disappearance? Or was it someone else entirely, someone closer to home?

"Is there anyone else who might have had a reason to harm Amelia?" He asked Hank, his voice low and urgent.

"Can't think of anyone off the top of my head," Hank replied, scratching his chin thoughtfully. "But you know how these things go, Jackson. Sometimes the people we least expect turn out to be the ones we should've been watching all along."

Jackson nodded, his eyes narrowing as he considered the implications of Hank's words. The sun had now set completely, leaving only the flickering lanterns to illuminate the dark corners of the ranch.

In the shadows, secrets lurked, waiting to be uncovered. And Jackson was more determined than ever to bring them into the light.

"Stay strong, Amelia," he thought, clenching his fists in silent resolve. "I'm getting closer. I promise."

The following morning, as the sun peeked over the horizon and bathed the Montgomery Ranch in a warm golden light, Jackson stood at the edge of the property, squinting into the distance. He took a deep breath, inhaling the scent of dew-drenched grass and fresh earth, trying to dispel the cloud of unease that hung over him.

"Mr. Turner!" a voice called from behind him. He turned to find Amelia's father, his face weary from another sleepless night.

"Mornin', Mr. Montgomery," Jackson replied, tipping his cowboy hat in greeting. "I've been going over everything we learned yesterday. There's something not quite right."

"Go on," Mr. Montgomery urged, his expression tightening with concern.

"Too many conflicting stories about Amelia's whereabouts before she disappeared," Jackson explained, running his fingers through his dark hair in frustration. "Some folks say they saw her down by the creek, while others insist she was riding out on the east range. We need to retrace her steps, figure out where the truth lies."

"Whatever it takes, Jackson," Mr. Montgomery said, his voice heavy with emotion. "Find my girl."

Determined, Jackson set out to unravel the tangled threads of Amelia's last known movements. But with each new lead he followed, the trail seemed to splinter further, leading him deeper into a maze of half-truths and dead ends.

"Maybe she went into town," suggested old Mrs. Jenkins, her arthritic hands clasped around a steaming cup of coffee. "I know she sometimes liked to visit the library there."

"Or perhaps she went to see that handsome young doctor," chimed in Sarah, the cook, a mischievous gleam in her eye. "He always had such a way of making her blush."

"Enough!" Jackson snapped, his patience wearing thin. "We're not getting anywhere with this."

"Sorry, Mr. Turner," Sarah muttered, her cheeks flushing with embarrassment. "I just thought... maybe it's something to consider."

As the day wore on, Jackson's frustration mounted. It was as though someone – or something – was actively working against him, throwing up roadblocks at every turn. If he didn't break through soon, he feared Amelia might slip further out of reach.

In a last-ditch effort, he decided to visit the old Thompson place, the last potential lead mentioned by the young ranch hand. The crumbling homestead stood like a ghostly relic from the past, its darkened windows staring silently across the windswept plains. As he approached, the hairs on the back of his neck prickled with unease.

"Amelia?" Jackson called out, his voice echoing through the empty rooms. "If you're here, give me a sign!"

Silence greeted him, and he sighed in disappointment. Another dead end.

Chapter 2: A Trail of Clues

The sun dipped low in the sky as Jackson rode up to the Montgomery Ranch, casting long shadows across the dusty landscape. The once-grand estate seemed to wither under the weight of Amelia's disappearance, her absence felt in every weathered board and fading rose bush. Jackson dismounted his horse, a sudden chill running down his spine despite the lingering warmth of the day.

"Amelia, where have you gone?" he whispered, his breath forming a small cloud in the cool air.

Taking a deep breath, Jackson strode toward the house, determination etched on his rugged face. He knew that if anyone could find Amelia, it was him. They shared a bond that went beyond friendship, a connection forged through years of laughter and heartache, adventure and quiet moments beneath the vast expanse of the Montana sky.

"Jackson!" called out Mrs. Montgomery, Amelia's mother, from the front porch, her voice hopeful. "Have you found something?"

"Not yet," Jackson replied, his voice gentle. "But I won't stop until I do."

With a nod of approval, she let him pass into the house, the heavy wooden door creaking shut behind him. As he climbed the stairs to Amelia's bedroom, he couldn't help but recall the countless times they had played hide-and-seek in these halls, the sound of their laughter echoing through the now-silent rooms.

Jackson hesitated at the entrance to Amelia's room, the familiar scent of lavender and leather filling his nostrils. Sunlight filtered through the lace curtains, casting dappled shadows on the floor as he stepped inside.

"Where could you be?" Jackson wondered aloud, his eyes scanning every corner of the room for any hint of her whereabouts. "What clue have you left behind?"

As he rummaged through her drawers, his fingers brushed against the delicate lace of her dresses, the silky strands of her hair ribbons, and the worn leather of her riding gloves. Each item sent a pang through his heart, a reminder of all the times they had shared together, as children and teenagers.

"Oh, Amelia," he muttered, frustration mounting as the minutes ticked by with no sign of a breakthrough. "I won't give up on you."

And with that promise echoing in the air, Jackson continued his search, fueled by memories of a girl with beautiful fiery red hair and a spirit that refused to be tamed. He would find Amelia, no matter what it took, and bring her back to the place where she truly belonged – the warm embrace of the Western sun, and the arms of the man who loved her.

As Jackson's search continued, the dimming light from the window flickered like a dying flame, casting eerie shadows across Amelia's bedroom. The silence of the room was broken only by the soft rustle of fabric as he moved through her belongings. A sudden gust of wind swept in, causing the curtains to dance wildly, and as they billowed outwards, something caught his eye.

"Amelia, you clever girl," he whispered as he approached the window. There, pinned beneath the heavy velvet drapes, was a slip of paper covered in what appeared to be a series of cryptic symbols. He carefully unpinned the message, feeling the weight of its importance settle on his shoulders.

"Alright, Amelia," he murmured, perching himself on the edge of her bed. "Let's see what secrets you've left for me."

He studied the symbols, his brow furrowed in concentration. Each symbol seemed to be a combination of letters and numbers, their meaning elusive. As the minutes stretched on, frustration settled in, but Jackson refused to become discouraged.

"What could it mean? You know Amelia better than anyone," he muttered to himself, his eyes never leaving the paper. Suddenly, it struck him – the symbols reminded him of a code they had devised as children, a secret language shared between kindred spirits.

"That's it!" Jackson exclaimed, his heart pounding with newfound determination. He began to decipher the hidden message, using the knowledge that only years of friendship could provide. Slowly but surely, the cryptic symbols transformed into words, forming a sentence that sent a shiver down his spine:

"Seek the canyon where echoes die, there lies the truth you must untie."

"Echoes..." Jackson murmured, his mind racing with possibilities. He knew that Amelia was drawn to the haunting beauty of the canyons, but which one held the key to her disappearance? As he pondered this question, his heart swelled with love and admiration for the woman who had left this clue. She was a force to be reckoned with, and he would stop at nothing to find her.

"Amelia," he whispered, clutching the decoded message tightly in his hand, "I won't fail you."

A gust of wind rattled the windowpane, sweeping away any lingering traces of warmth as Jackson studied the message anew. His eyes darted across the room, eventually landing on the dusty bookshelf where a worn leather-bound atlas rested. He walked over and opened it, eager to pinpoint the canyon that held Amelia's secrets. A torn page served as a bookmark. Jackson opened the page and saw that it was a map.

"Seek the canyon where echoes die," he repeated, running his fingers through his dark, tousled hair as he studied the map. The words danced in his mind, painting images of towering cliffs and shadowy crevices, their depths veiled in mystery. As he closed the atlas, he could almost hear Amelia's soft laughter, a sound that once filled these canyons with life and joy. Now, those echoes were silenced – but not for long, if he had any say in it.

"Have you found something?" a soft voice asked from the doorway, startling him. It was Mrs. Montgomery, her eyes red-rimmed from crying.

"I believe so," Jackson replied. "Amelia left a map. I'm going to follow it."

"Please, bring her back to us," Mrs. Montgomery implored, her voice trembling with emotion.

"Trust me, ma'am," Jackson reassured her, his gaze never wavering. "I'll move heaven and earth to find her."

With renewed determination, he set about gathering his supplies: food and water, a sturdy rope, a reliable compass, and an array of tools that would serve him well in the wilderness. In his mind, he envisioned the treacherous journey ahead – the steep inclines, the narrow passages, the relentless sun beating down upon him – but none of these obstacles would stop him. They were merely challenges to be overcome.

"Time to saddle up," Jackson murmured, his steely resolve mirrored in the glint of his hazel eyes. There was still hope, and as long as that ember burned within his heart, he would do everything in his power to bring her home.

"Amelia," he whispered once more, a promise hanging in the air as he prepared to embark on the greatest adventure of his life. "Just hold on a little longer."

The sun dipped low in the sky, casting a warm glow on the rugged landscape as Jackson carefully studied the torn piece of the map he had discovered in Amelia's bedroom. He traced his fingers over the faded ink, feeling the rough texture of the parchment beneath his fingertips. The remote canyon was marked with a small 'X,' but the surrounding landmarks were only vaguely drawn, making it difficult to pinpoint its exact location.

"Well look at that," he muttered under his breath, frustration creeping into the furrow of his brow. He knew that every second counted, and the vague markings on the map only added to the urgency clawing at his chest.

With a determined sigh, he folded the map and tucked it securely into his pocket before making his way to the nearby saloon, where locals often gathered to share stories and trade information. The sound of raucous laughter and lively piano music spilled out into the dusty street as he pushed open the creaky door, stepping into the dimly lit establishment.

"Evenin', stranger," drawled the grizzled bartender as Jackson approached the bar. "What can I do for you?"

"Got any folk around here who know the lay of the land?" Jackson asked. "I'm lookin' for some help findin' a particular canyon."

"Reckon old Jasper might be able to help you," the bartender replied, nodding toward a hunched figure in the corner, his gnarled hands wrapped around a mug of ale. "He knows these parts like the back of his hand."

"Much obliged," Jackson said, tipping his hat before approaching the wizened man. The smell of tobacco smoke clung to the air around him as he took a seat next to Jasper, swallowing hard against the rising tide of anxiety within him.

"Jasper, is it?" Jackson began, extending a calloused hand in greeting. "I'm Jackson Turner. I've heard you know these parts better than anyone, and I could use your expertise."

"Depends on what you're after," Jasper replied gruffly, his eyes narrowing in suspicion.

"Lookin' for a canyon. A remote one," Jackson explained, pulling the torn map from his pocket and unfolding it for Jasper to see. "There's somethin' important I need to find there."

Jasper studied the map carefully, his gnarled fingers tracing the lines as he hummed thoughtfully. "Looks like Dead Man's Canyon, if I ain't mistaken," he finally declared, tapping the 'X' with a calloused finger. "But it ain't a place for the faint of heart, son. Treacherous terrain, unpredictable weather, and more than a few unsavory characters call that place home."

"Believe me, I ain't takin' this journey lightly," Jackson admitted, his thoughts turning to Amelia and the desperate need to find her. "But I've got no choice. There's someone who needs my help."

"Then you best be prepared for what you'll face out there," Jasper warned, his voice low and grave. "You'll need all your wits about you, and then some."

"Thank you, Jasper," Jackson said solemnly, the weight of his mission settling heavily upon his shoulders. "I intend to see this through."

The sun dipped low on the horizon, casting a warm golden hue over the landscape as Jackson mounted his trusty mare with determination in every line of his body. He couldn't shake the feeling that time was running out, and if he didn't reach Amelia soon, it might be too late.

"Remember, son," Jasper called out from the steps of the saloon as Jackson prepared to ride off. "Keep your eyes open and follow your instincts."

"Trust me, I will," Jackson replied, tipping his hat in gratitude before nudging his horse into a steady trot. As the saloon disappeared behind him, he felt the weight of his mission pressing down upon him like a heavy saddlebag.

The journey began through familiar terrain, but as the miles passed, the landscape grew increasingly rugged and wild. The well-trodden paths gave way to rocky trails and steep inclines, forcing Jackson and Butterscotch to navigate carefully through the treacherous footing. With each challenge overcome, Jackson's thoughts turned to Amelia – her laugh, her smile, her fire – fueling his resolve to face whatever obstacles lay ahead.

As they climbed higher into the mountains, the air grew colder and thin, causing both man and horse to labor for breath. At times, the narrow trail skirted along sheer cliffs, leaving little room for error. One misstep could send them plummeting into oblivion, but Jackson's focus never wavered. He knew that Amelia was depending on him, and he would not fail her.

"Come on, girl," he murmured to Butterscotch, urging her on with gentle encouragement. "We're almost there. We can do this."

But as if the treacherous terrain wasn't enough, the weather seemed determined to thwart their progress. Dark clouds rolled in, bringing with them biting winds and sudden bursts of rain that pelted Jackson's face like a thousand tiny needles. His soaked clothes clung to him, chilling him to the bone, but he refused to give in to the cold and discomfort.

"Amelia's counting on me," he reminded himself, gritting his teeth against the wind. "Can't let a little rain stop me now."

As they pushed onward, Jackson couldn't shake the feeling that they were being watched. It was an unsettling sensation, as though eyes were constantly following his every move. He caught glimpses of movement out of the corner of his eye – shadows darting between trees, rustling branches just beyond his line of sight – but when he turned to look, there was nothing there.

"Must be the nerves gettin' to me," he muttered under his breath, trying to ignore the prickling sensation at the back of his neck.

But then, as he rounded a bend in the trail, he found himself face to face with a snarling wolf, its fur bristling and teeth bared in a menacing growl. Jackson's heart clenched in his chest, adrenaline surging through him like wildfire.

"Easy, girl," he whispered to his horse, keeping his voice low and steady as he reached for his sidearm. "Just stay calm, and we'll get through this."

The standoff seemed to stretch on for an eternity, the wolf's yellow eyes boring into Jackson's soul as it weighed its options. Then, with a final warning growl, the creature backed away slowly before disappearing into the underbrush.

"Whew," Jackson breathed, holstering his pistol and releasing a long-held breath. With renewed urgency, he urged his horse forward, knowing that Amelia was still out there somewhere, waiting for him to find her. And he would not – could not – let her down.

The sun dipped low in the sky, casting long shadows across the rocky landscape as Jackson made his way towards the remote canyon. His body ached from the grueling journey, but the ache was a distant thought compared to the mounting dread that filled him with each step he took closer to Amelia's possible whereabouts.

"Focus, Jack," he muttered to himself, scanning the terrain for any hint of danger. "You've faced worse than this before." He was used to the rugged life of a cowboy, and the open frontier was where he felt most at home. Being out in the vast untamed beauty of the wild west gave him a sense of freedom and brought peace to his spirit.

A sudden gust of icy wind whipped at his face, carrying with it the scent of rain and the promise of a brewing storm. He pulled his hat down tighter against the onslaught, urging Butterscotch onward as they travelled the path leading to the canyon.

"Almost there, girl," he reassured his horse, patting her neck gently. "Just a little further."

As they climbed, the path grew steeper, with jagged rocks jutting out at odd angles and threatening to send them both plummeting into the abyss below. Jackson relied on his instincts and years of experience in the wild to navigate the perilous ascent, all the while keeping his eyes peeled for any sign of Amelia.

"Amelia," he whispered under his breath, as though saying her name would conjure her up before him. "Please be here. Please be safe."

At last, as the first drops of rain began to fall from the sky, Jackson and his horse crested the rise and found themselves staring at the edge of a remote canyon. The sight that greeted him was both breathtaking and terrifying – a vast chasm that seemed to stretch on forever, its depths shrouded in shadow and mystery.

Chapter 3: The Mysterious Stranger

"Alright, Amelia," Jackson whispered to himself. "I'll follow your trail, wherever it may lead."

He found himself lost in thought, reflecting on his connection with the auburn-haired beauty. Their shared past, the unspoken bond that had always lingered between them – it all seemed to be converging on this single moment, as if fate itself had conspired to guide him to her side.

"Can't let you down now, can I?" he mused, giving his horse a gentle nudge. "We've got a long road ahead of us."

As they ventured further, dust swirled around them, whipped up by the wind that swept across the desolate landscape.

"Wait for me, Amelia," he whispered into the wind, his words carried away by the desert breeze. "I'm coming for you."

Jackson's silhouette disappeared into the distant shadows of the remote canyon, guided by the strength of his love and the promise of a mystery yet unsolved.

As he guided his horse around a bend in the rocky terrain, the sun dipped lower on the horizon, casting long shadows that seemed to reach out and dance across the path before him. The air was heavy with an eerie silence, pierced only by the distant cries of coyotes echoing through the canyon's depths. His pulse quickened as he felt the first tendrils of suspense curling up from the pit of his stomach.

"Easy, girl," Jackson murmured to Butterscotch, patting her muscular neck reassuringly. He squinted into the distance, straining his eyes against the fading light until they fell upon a figure up ahead – a man on horseback, emerging from the dusky haze like a specter.

"Evenin'," the stranger called out as he approached, the brim of his hat casting shadows over the angular features of his face. "Name's Ethan Reynolds."

"Jackson Turner," he replied cautiously, his grip tightening on the reins. Deep within him, instinct screamed out a warning, but curiosity held him fast.

"Seems we're headed the same way," Ethan said, his voice smooth and low. "I heard word you're lookin' for Amelia Montgomery. Reckon I could lend a hand."

"Is that so?" Jackson's gaze never left the stranger's face, searching for any hint of deception. A thousand questions raced through his mind. Who was this man, and what did he know of Amelia's disappearance? Could he be trusted?

"Truth is, Mr. Turner, Amelia saved my life once," Ethan confessed, fixing him with a piercing stare. "I owe her a debt. And I aim to repay it by helpin' you find her."

For a moment, the world seemed to stand still – the whisper of wind through the sagebrush, the distant call of the coyotes, even the steady breathing of their horses fading away as Jackson weighed his options. Was it fate that had brought them together on this desolate stretch of land, or was it something darker?

"Alright, Ethan," he finally said, exhaling a breath he hadn't realized he'd been holding. "We'll ride together."

"Much obliged," Ethan replied, tipping his hat with a nod. And as the sun dipped below the horizon, casting the world into darkness, the two men rode side by side.

"Amelia," thought Jackson, his heart heavy. "Hold on. We're coming for you."

The moon hung low in the sky, casting eerie shadows on the rugged terrain as Jackson and Ethan rode along. Each man lost in his thoughts, the silence between them was charged with tension. Finally, Jackson couldn't hold it in any longer.

"Tell me, Ethan," he began, his voice barely audible above the rhythmic clip-clop of their horses' hooves. "What do you know about Amelia's disappearance?"

Ethan hesitated for a moment, as if gathering his thoughts, before responding. "Well, I reckon it ain't much, but there's talk in town about her bein' seen near Dead Man's Canyon where we're headed towards."

"Rumors?" Jackson frowned, his heart pounding with a mix of hope and fear. "Who's been sayin' such things?"

"Can't rightly say who started the whispers," Ethan admitted, his expression somber. "But word travels fast 'round these parts, and folks are sayin' she was spotted not too long ago, accompanied by someone they didn't recognize."

"Someone?" The question hung heavy in the air, and Jackson couldn't help but cast a sidelong glance at Ethan – this stranger who had inserted himself into Amelia's life, and now his own.

"See, that's the thing," Ethan continued, sensing Jackson's growing suspicion. "No one knows who this person might be. Could be friend or foe. But it's the only lead we got, and it's better than ridin' blind, don't you think?"

"Suppose you're right," Jackson conceded, his eyes narrowing as they scanned the horizon. "So, what's our plan of action?"

"First, we'll follow Amelia's trail to Dead Man's Canyon," Ethan replied, his voice tinged with determination. "Once we get there, we'll scout around, see if we can find any sign of her – or this mysterious companion."

"Sounds like a plan," Jackson agreed, his grip tightening on the reins as they pressed forward into the moonlit night.

"Listen, Jackson," Ethan said, his voice softening with sincerity. "I know you got your doubts about me, and I don't blame you. But I truly want to help you find Amelia. She means a lot to me, too."

Jackson nodded slowly, acknowledging Ethan's words but not yet ready to truly trust him. "We'll see, Ethan. We'll see."

And with that, the two men rode on through the dark, their shared objective forging a tentative alliance between them. Yet, as the miles passed beneath their horses' hooves, Jackson couldn't shake the uneasy feeling that had settled in his gut, like a rattlesnake coiled and ready to strike. Was it merely the uncertainty of their quest that weighed on him, or was there something more sinister at play?

"Amelia," he thought, his heart swelling with a mixture of love and dread. "Wherever you are, we're gettin' closer. Just hold on."

***

The first light of dawn cast a golden glow over the rugged landscape as Jackson and Ethan packed up camp from the night before and prepared for the day's journey. Their horses snorted impatiently, sensing the urgency in their masters' movements. Jackson adjusted the saddle on Butterscotch, while Ethan meticulously checked the supplies they'd hastily gathered from town. They'd gotten food and water to sustain them and their horses, as well as ropes and lanterns for navigating the treacherous canyon terrain.

"Looks like we've got everything," said Ethan, wiping the sweat from his brow. "We should make good time today."

"Let's hope so," Jackson replied, mounting Butterscotch with practiced ease. He couldn't help but feel the weight of Amelia's fate pressing down on him, driving him to push onward at an unrelenting pace.

As they set off towards Dead Man's Canyon, the sun rose higher in the sky, casting long shadows across the dusty plains. The air was thick with anticipation, and Jackson found himself stealing glances at Ethan, trying to figure out this strange new ally. Was he truly here to help, or was there some hidden agenda lurking behind those dark eyes?

"Y'know, I never pegged you as the talkative type," Ethan drawled, catching Jackson's gaze. "Or is it just my charm leavin' you speechless?"

"Maybe I'm just tryin' to figure you out," Jackson admitted, cracking a smile despite himself. "You're quite the mystery, Ethan Reynolds."

"Reckon I could say the same about you," Ethan replied, his grin revealing a hint of vulnerability. "But I suppose now's as good a time as any to get acquainted."

Over the course of their journey, the two men engaged in conversation, and as the miles rolled by, they discovered shared interests, slowly building trust and forming a bond that surprised them both.

"Never thought I'd be ridin' alongside Jackson Turner," Ethan mused that evening as they made camp beneath a blanket of stars. "Not after the way we met, anyway."

"Can't say I ever imagined it either," Jackson agreed, staring into the flickering fire. "But here we are, two lost souls tryin' to find their way through this tangled mess."

"Seems like fate has a funny way of bringin' folks together," Ethan remarked.

"Maybe so," Jackson conceded, with a newfound appreciation for this new friend. "Maybe so."

But as much as he wanted to let down his guard completely, Jackson couldn't shake the lingering doubts that whispered in the back of his mind as he drifted off to sleep. Was Ethan hiding something? Could he truly trust him?

***

The morning sunrise cast a golden glow over the rugged landscape as Jackson and Ethan approached Dead Man's Canyon. The shadows of the towering rock formations grew longer, stretching out like an omen that sent a shiver down Jackson's spine.

"Should be there by nightfall," Ethan announced, his gaze locked on the horizon.

"Yup," Jackson replied, his voice tense with unease. Their bond had grown stronger throughout their journey, but now, as they neared their destination, he couldn't help but feel the familiar weight of suspicion returning to his chest.

"Somethin' the matter?" Ethan asked, genuine concern painted across his face.

"What do you really know about this canyon? Why were you so eager to help me find Amelia?" Jackson asked. He'd always been a loner, not depending on anybody but himself. It was a new feeling having this companion on the journey to the canyon.

Ethan hesitated for a moment, then sighed deeply, as if preparing himself for a confession. "You deserve to know the truth, Jackson," he began, his voice steady and sincere. "My sister, Clara, went missin' 'round these parts some five years back. Nobody ever found her, or even knew what happened to her. When I heard about Amelia, I couldn't just stand by. Not again."

Jackson's eyes widened, taken aback by Ethan's words. He studied the lines of the man's face, searching for any hint of deception, but found only sincerity shining through the pain.

"Reckon we've both lost someone important to us," Jackson said softly, his own heart aching at the thought of Amelia. "I'm sorry about your sister, Ethan. I truly am."

"Thank you, Jackson. I appreciate that," Ethan replied, his voice heavy with emotion. "Now you know why I'm here, why I want to help. It ain't just about Amelia. It's about finding closure for all of us."

"Alright," Jackson said, swallowing hard as he pushed aside his lingering doubts. "Let's find them both."

As they continued their journey, the sun dipped below the horizon, plunging the canyon into darkness. The air turned colder, and a sense of foreboding settled over the land. But even as the shadows deepened and the wind howled through the rocks, Jackson felt a newfound resolve coursing through his veins. With every step closer to the canyon, he was one step closer to finding Amelia – and perhaps, just maybe, bringing peace to Ethan's tormented soul as well.

***

The first light of dawn painted the canyon walls in a palette of warm hues, casting long shadows on the rocky ground. As they made their way further into Dead Man's Canyon, Jackson led their horses by the reins, his boots crunching on the soil. He glanced sideways at Ethan, who walked beside him, seemingly lost in thought.

"Beautiful, ain't it?" Jackson remarked, nodding towards the breathtaking scenery.

"Sure is," Ethan agreed, his voice soft and distant. "Makes you feel small, don't it? Like there's so much more to this world than just our own little troubles."

"Reckon that's true," Jackson mused, his gaze lingering on the morning light dancing across the canyon walls. But despite the beauty surrounding them, his thoughts were consumed by Amelia, her beautiful face a constant presence in his mind. He couldn't shake the feeling that they were running out of time – that every moment they spent searching for her was another moment she might be slipping further away.

As they continued onwards, Jackson couldn't help but keep a watchful eye on Ethan, still unsure about the man's true intentions. Ethan had shared the story of his sister and the pain he carried, but there remained something unsettling about him. A nagging doubt whispered in the back of Jackson's mind, urging caution.

"Need a break?" Ethan asked, halting as he noticed Jackson's weary expression.

"Maybe just a quick one," Jackson replied, wiping the sweat from his brow. They tethered their horses to a nearby tree and settled down on a large boulder, pulling canteens from their saddlebags.

"Y'know, I've been thinkin'," Ethan said, taking a swig from his canteen before turning to Jackson with a serious expression. "If we find Amelia, if we bring her back safe and sound... what then?"

"Then we go on with our lives, I suppose," Jackson answered, his heart pounding at the mere mention of Amelia's name. "Amelia goes back to her family, and I... I go back to the life of a cowboy."

"Is that what you want?" Ethan pressed, his dark eyes searching Jackson's face. "To just go back to how things were?"

"Maybe not everything," Jackson admitted, his thoughts drifting towards the unspoken feelings he harbored for Amelia. "But that's a bridge we'll cross when we come to it."

"Fair enough," Ethan said, nodding in agreement. "I just hope we find her soon."

"Me too," Jackson replied, his determination renewed.

As they resumed their search, Jackson remained vigilant, the weight of responsibility heavy on his shoulders. He had promised himself that he would find her, no matter the cost. And despite the uncertainty gnawing at him, he knew that he couldn't afford to let doubt cloud his judgment.

Chapter 4: Secrets of the Montgomery's

The sun dipped low behind the distant hills, casting a golden glow across the sprawling Montgomery Ranch. Jackson's boots crunched upon the gravel driveway, his eyes scanning the homestead before him. He and Ethan had parted ways after a few days of searching Dead Man's Canyon with no luck, and Jackson had returned to Amelia's home to try to find another clue to her puzzling disappearance.

"Thank you for coming, Jackson," said Mrs. Montgomery, as she opened the door. "We're all quite worried, and we appreciate your help."

Jackson nodded, his thoughts consumed by Amelia's soft laughter and warm green eyes. He felt a fierce determination rise within him, fueled by their shared childhood memories and undeniable connection. "Not a trace of her at the canyon, ma'am. Maybe I can find something here that will help."

As he stepped inside the old ranch, the shadows of the late afternoon cast eerie patterns on the walls. Jackson began exploring each room, searching for any clue that might lead him to Amelia. His heart raced at every creak and whisper, the tension palpable in every corner of the massive house.

"Amelia," he whispered under his breath, as though saying her name aloud might conjure her into existence. "Where are you?"

An hour passed, and Jackson found himself climbing the grand staircase to the attic, flashlight in hand, drawn by an inexplicable sense of urgency. The dusty air filled his nostrils and made him cough, but he couldn't shake the feeling that there was something important hidden within the dimly lit confines of the space.

As Jackson rummaged through the cluttered attic, his fingers brushed against a cold metal latch. Curiosity piqued, he pulled it, revealing a cleverly concealed entrance to a hidden room. The door creaked open, sending a shiver down his spine.

"Well, what have we here?" he muttered, stepping cautiously into the musty chamber. Jackson couldn't help but feel a mixture of excitement and dread.

"Amelia," he whispered again, the word now tinted with both hope and fear. If Amelia was hiding something in this room, could it be the key to her disappearance?

As Jackson stood at the threshold of the hidden room, the weight of his responsibility loomed heavy on his shoulders. Every step he took would bring him closer not only to the truth about Amelia's fate but also to the tangled web of deception that had ensnared her family for generations.

"Enough!" he said aloud, steeling himself against the uncertainty that threatened to overwhelm him. "I'll find you, Amelia. No matter what it takes." And with those words, Jackson stepped into the shadows, ready to face whatever secrets lay within.

The air in the hidden room was thick with the smell of dust and age, as if the very walls breathed the secrets they contained. Jackson's eyes adjusted to the dim light that spilled through the narrow window, revealing rows of wooden shelves laden with old books and papers, their covers worn and faded.

"Hello there," he murmured, reaching out to gingerly trace his fingers along the spines of the ancient volumes. He could almost feel the pulse of the past beneath his fingertips, each book a vessel for the echoes of stories long forgotten.

Jackson's hand came to rest on a stack of leather-bound journals, their pages yellowed and brittle with age. He hesitated for a moment, then carefully lifted one from the pile and opened it, taking care not to damage the fragile paper. As he scanned the faded ink, his heart raced at the realization that these were the personal accounts of generations of Montgomery's, their intimate thoughts and experiences laid bare on the page.

"Amelia," he whispered, his voice a mix of longing and determination as his thoughts were consumed with her. If the answers he sought lay within these pages, then he would uncover them, no matter the cost.

As he read through the journals, Jackson became lost in a world of whispered confessions and veiled accusations, feeling the weight of the Montgomery family's secrets press down upon him like a blanket. With each entry, he uncovered a history of betrayal that spanned generations, with shocking revelations about past conflicts and hidden agendas that left him reeling.

"Son of a gun," he muttered, shaking his head in disbelief.

A sudden gust of wind rattled the window, sending shivers down Jackson's spine as if the ghosts of the past had taken offense at his intrusion. He gritted his teeth, his jaw set with determination, and continued to dive into the dark corners of the Montgomery family history.

"Jackson..." Amelia's voice seemed to echo in his mind, the memory of her laughter mingling with the howling wind. It was as if she were there beside him, urging him on in his quest for the truth.

With each page he turned, Jackson became more and more immersed in the tangled web of deceit that had ensnared his childhood friend. The room seemed to close in around him, the musty air thick with secrets and betrayal, but he refused to be discouraged. He hoped that somewhere within these pages lay the key to Amelia's disappearance.

Jackson flipped to a journal entry dated several years prior. The handwriting grew shaky and erratic, as if the author had been consumed by emotion while penning the words.

"Amelia's father...and Samuel Caldwell?" he whispered to himself, his brow furrowing in confusion. "What in the world could they be fightin' about?"

As he continued reading, the details of the decades-old feud between the two men began to unravel before him. Greed, jealousy, and a thirst for power all seemed to fuel the bitter rivalry that had long plagued the Montgomery family.

"Hmmm," Jackson muttered, his heart pounding in his chest. "Could Mr. Caldwell be responsible for Amelia's disappearance?"

He could feel the curiosity rising within him like a wildfire, as his mind raced and his grip tightened around the leather-bound journal.

"Amelia, what have you gotten yourself into?" he thought, despair creeping into the edges of his determination.

"Jackson," a soft voice called out from behind him. He turned to see the shimmering apparition of Amelia, her eyes filled with tears.

"Amelia!" he cried, reaching out to touch her, but his hand passed through her like a phantom. "I'll find you, darlin'. I promise."

"Find the truth, Jackson," she whispered before fading away, leaving him alone with the weight of the Montgomery family secrets pressing down upon him.

"Truth..." he murmured into the cold air, his breath visible in the dim light. He looked back at the journal, the words swimming before his eyes as he tried to piece together the story hidden beneath layers of deception.

"Samuel Caldwell, you're gonna pay if you've done something to Amelia," he vowed, his voice low and steady.

With renewed determination, Jackson studied the journals, fueled by a burning desire to uncover the truth and rescue Amelia.

"How deep does this go?" Jackson whispered, feeling the weight of the revelations press down on his chest. The scent of old parchment and aging leather filled his nostrils, only adding to the suffocating tension that hung heavy in the air.

"Father was right," he read aloud from an entry penned in shaky handwriting. "Samuel Caldwell is not who he seems. I must confront him before it's too late." Jackson clenched his jaw, anger sparking within him at the thought of Samuel's possible role in Amelia's disappearance.

"What have you done, Samuel Caldwell?" he growled, flipping to another page. There, he found a passage detailing a clandestine meeting between Amelia's father and Samuel. They had argued, the words heated and laced with venom.

"Amelia, did you know about this feud?" Jackson wondered, his heart aching at the idea that she had been caught in the crossfire between her father and Samuel Caldwell.

He could almost feel the warmth of her breath ghosting across his skin as he pictured her pleading eyes searching for comfort in his own.

"Amelia darlin', you just hold on," he murmured. "I'll find you, and I'll put an end to this once and for all."

He continued scouring the journals, each one shedding more light onto the twisted history of the Montgomery family. His resolve strengthened with every word he read, fueling the fire of his determination to save Amelia and bring justice to those who had wronged her.

"Time is running out," he reminded himself. He hoped that the answers were there, hidden within the pages of the journals, waiting to be unearthed.

The air in the hidden room seemed to grow heavier with every turn of a page, as though the weight of secrets sought to suffocate Jackson. He felt a mix of anger and sadness for the Montgomery family, but above all else, a fierce determination to bring justice to those who had caused Amelia's disappearance.

"Samuel Caldwell... you're up to your neck in this," Jackson muttered under his breath, holding onto the worn leather journal that contained the nefarious connection. As he explored its pages, he discovered that Samuel had been involved in the disappearance of another Montgomery family member years ago – Amelia's aunt. It was a chilling revelation, one that sent shivers down Jackson's spine and set his heart racing.

"You won't get away with this," he vowed, his voice a low growl that filled the room. He couldn't forget Amelia's laughter and the way her eyes sparkled in the sunlight. They were memories that fueled his determination to save her.

"Amelia, wherever you are, I'll find you," Jackson whispered into the shadows, promising himself that he would unravel the mystery surrounding her disappearance and bring those responsible to justice.

Jackson's hand shook slightly as he turned another page, revealing more of the Montgomery family's twisted history. Each sentence, each word, added fuel to the fire burning inside him, solidifying his resolve to bring those responsible for Amelia's disappearance to justice.

"Can't believe it..." he muttered, shaking his head in disbelief.

As he continued to explore the yellowed pages, Jackson's thoughts drifted to their childhood together, when life was simpler, and the weight of her family's treachery had not yet overshadowed Amelia's laughter. He remembered the way her eyes shone like stars on moonlit nights when they'd sneak away from their respective homes to share secret dreams and stolen kisses beneath the vast Montana sky.

"Justice will be served," he vowed, his voice firm and resolute. "No matter the cost."

"Samuel Caldwell," he murmured, gripping the journal tightly, his knuckles turning white. "The pieces are falling into place, and your time is running out."

For just a moment, Jackson allowed himself to imagine what it would be like to confront the man who had torn apart not only Amelia's family but also his own heart. He could almost feel the cold steel of the revolver in his hand and hear the words he'd say.

"Your reign of terror ends here," he whispered, as if speaking directly to Samuel Caldwell himself.

The final words of the last journal echoed in Jackson's mind as he snapped it shut, a cloud of dust billowing up from its ancient pages. "And so, the cycle of betrayal continues." He sat back on his heels, surrounded by the leather-bound testimonies of generations long gone, each one weighed down by secrets and lies.

"Jackson!" A muffled shout came from somewhere below, causing him to startle. It was Amelia's younger brother, Robert. "Where are you?" The urgency in Robert's voice stirred Jackson into action.

"Coming!" he called out, hastily gathering the journals and stacking them neatly on a dusty shelf.

"Wait just a little longer, Amelia," he thought, his hand brushing over the concealed door as he stepped out of the hidden chamber. "I swear, I'll bring you home."

"Jackson, did you find anything?" Robert asked when they met in the hallway, his eyes filled with curiosity.

"Sure," Jackson replied, forcing a smile. "I got caught up in some old memories while searching the attic." His fingertips rested against the door, feeling the cool metal of the lock as he turned it, securing the secrets within. "I'm not giving up."

"Neither am I," Robert affirmed, placing a hand on Jackson's shoulder.

"Good," Jackson agreed, though his thoughts were already racing ahead, fueled by the knowledge locked away in the hidden room.

"Rest well tonight, Samuel Caldwell," he thought, his eyes narrowing with resolve. "Soon, you'll answer for your sins." And with that, Jackson followed Robert down the dimly lit hallway towards the dining room where dinner awaited, the whispers of betrayal and revenge echoing like ghostly footsteps behind him.

***

The sun had long since dipped below the horizon, and a blanket of darkness enveloped the Montgomery Ranch. In the distance, the silhouette of the house stood tall against the starry sky, its windows casting pools of golden light onto the earth below. Jackson stepped outside onto the porch and took a deep breath, inhaling the cool night air that carried with it the faint scent of sagebrush.

"Can't sleep, Jackson?" Robert called out from a rocking chair, his cowboy hat casting a shadow over his face.

"Too much on my mind," Jackson admitted, his gaze fixed on the far-off mountains that seemed to hold secrets of their own. "I can't shake the feeling that time is running out for Amelia."

"I know what you mean," Robert agreed. He paused, looking back at the ranch. "I just wish we had more to go on."

"Maybe we do," Jackson said quietly, recalling the memories he'd uncovered in the hidden room. His heart beat faster as the weight of the family's dark past pressed down on him, but he knew he couldn't reveal the secret just yet—not until he understood how it all connected to Amelia's disappearance.

"Robert," Jackson began cautiously, "Have you ever heard of Samuel Caldwell?"

"Samuel Caldwell?" Robert furrowed his brow, searching his memory. "Yeah, that name sounds familiar, but I can't place where I've heard it before."

"Keep an eye out for any mention of him," Jackson instructed. "I have a feeling he's involved in all this somehow."

"Alright, I'll remember that," Robert agreed, nodding slowly.

"Good," Jackson said, clenching his fists. "I can't help but feel that Amelia's fate and the past are intertwined somehow." He hesitated, then added softly, "I just wish I could protect her from it all."

"Jackson, you've always been there for her—ever since we were kids," Robert reminded him, a hint of warmth in his voice. "You're doing everything you can to find her. And when she's back safe and sound, she'll know that she can rely on you."

"Thanks, Robert," Jackson murmured, touched by his friend's words. He knew he couldn't afford to let his emotions consume him—not when Amelia needed him most. With newfound resolve, he straightened his shoulders and resolved to fight the darkness that had entangled the Montgomery's.

"Let's get some rest," Robert said with a yawn.

"Alright," Jackson replied, as they turned and headed back inside the ranch. The lingering scent of sagebrush seemed to whisper a promise of secrets yet to be discovered—and justice yet to be served.

Chapter 5: Ranch Troubles

The sun hung low in the sky, casting amber rays across the dusty landscape as Jackson rode up to the Montgomery Ranch. The air was heavy with the scent of dry earth and impending trouble.

As he approached, the front door swung open, revealing Amelia's father, a tall, gaunt man with deep-set eyes that seemed to carry the weight of a thousand sorrows. His face was lined with the unmistakable marks left by worry and sleepless nights. "Jackson," he said, his voice cracked with emotion.

"Mr. Montgomery," Jackson replied, dismounting his horse with grace. He quickly strode up the steps to meet the older gentleman, concern etched upon his face. "What's going on?"

"Come inside," Amelia's father beckoned, leading Jackson through the familiar halls of the house, now marred by tension. As they entered the study, he poured two glasses of whiskey, handing one to Jackson before taking a deep sip from his own. "Jackson, I've uncovered something I never thought I'd have to face."

"Tell me," Jackson urged, his eyes searching the careworn man's face for answers.

"I've discovered that we're on the brink of ruin," Mr. Montgomery admitted, his voice barely above a whisper.

"Ruin?" Jackson echoed, his brow furrowing as he struggled to comprehend the words.

"Debts, Jackson. Debts that got out of hand," the older man continued, his voice trembling with the weight of his confession. "I don't know how it got this bad, but if we don't find a way to settle them, we'll lose everything."

Jackson looked around the study, memories of laughter and love filling his mind as he took in the room's fading grandeur. He could see Amelia in every corner, her fiery spirit igniting the very air around her.

"Mr. Montgomery," Jackson began, his eyes locked onto those of the man who had always been like a second father to him. "We'll get through this. We'll find Amelia, and we'll save the ranch. I promise you."

A heavy silence settled over the room as Jackson's words hung in the air, a solemn promise that seemed to strengthen the resolve in Mr. Montgomery's eyes. The older man cleared his throat and nodded, extending a hand to clasp Jackson's shoulder firmly.

"Thank you, son. I know Amelia would be grateful for your help," he said, his voice thick with emotion.

Determined to get to the bottom of the ranch's financial troubles, Jackson rolled up his sleeves and squared his shoulders. "First things first, we need to understand the situation better. Is there someone who can give me an overview of the accounts?"

"Our accountant, Richard, is here and should be able to provide details," Mr. Montgomery replied, directing Jackson out of the study and down the dimly lit hallway adorned with family portraits. The scent of dust and old leather filled Jackson's nostrils, reminding him of countless days spent poring over books or exchanging stories in this once lively home.

The door to the small office creaked open to reveal Richard, a middle-aged man with thinning hair and a perpetually furrowed brow. At their entrance, he looked up from the stack of papers weighing down the desk, his gaze flickering between Mr. Montgomery and Jackson.

"Jackson is here to help us sort through these financial issues. Can you give him an overview of our situation?" Mr. Montgomery asked, his voice betraying a hint of desperation.

"Of course," Richard responded hesitantly, adjusting his spectacles as he turned to face Jackson. "It won't be easy to hear, but I'll do my best."

Jackson pulled up a chair beside Richard and leaned in, bracing himself for the unpleasant truths that awaited him. As Richard began to outline the extent of the debt, Jackson felt a knot tighten in his stomach. It was worse than he had imagined. The numbers danced before him like a sinister waltz, each figure a reminder of the danger that loomed over the Montgomery family.

"We've got to find a way to turn this around," Jackson muttered.

"Indeed," Richard agreed, his eyes downcast. "But I fear it will take more than just hard work and determination. We need a miracle."

"Miracles have a funny way of showing up when you least expect them," Jackson said with a determined smile. He was no stranger to adversity and had faced it down more times than he could count. This time would be no different.

"Well," the accountant continued, "as you can see, the ranch has been struggling to make ends meet due to a combination of low cattle prices and mounting debts." A thick ledger lay open before them, its pages filled with neat columns of numbers that told a grim tale.

Jackson's jaw tightened as he took in the figures. This was worse than he'd imagined. He could feel the weight of the situation pressing down on him, but he refused to let it break his resolve. Amelia needed him now more than ever, and he would do whatever it took to save her family's ranch.

"We need to explore potential solutions. What if we were to secure a loan or find new business opportunities for the ranch? There must be something we can do," said Jackson.

Richard looked thoughtful for a moment, then replied, "A loan might provide temporary relief, but without a steady source of income, we'll find ourselves back in this same predicament before long. As for new business opportunities... well, it's worth exploring what options are available."

Jackson leaned back in his chair, eyes fixed on the wallpaper. Amelia's sweet laughter echoed in his memory, and he knew he couldn't afford to fail her. His mind raced as he considered every possibility that might present itself.

"Richard, I want you to look into any and all options for loans," Jackson instructed, his voice steady and determined. "Meanwhile, I'll start asking around about possible business ventures. We can't be the only ones struggling in these difficult times. Maybe there are others who would be willing to work with us."

"Absolutely," Richard replied, giving a solemn nod. "I'll do my utmost to find a solution."

"Thank you," Jackson said as he stood up. His thoughts turned again to Amelia as he left the room. Saving the ranch was just one piece of the puzzle, but it was a crucial one. He'd find her, he vowed silently, and together they would restore the Montgomery Ranch to its former glory.

The wind carried a faint scent of rain, a promise of respite from the heat as Jackson prepared to ride out in search of answers. He tightened the cinch on his saddle, feeling the weight of responsibility settle on his shoulders like the dust that clung to his boots.

As he swung into the saddle, Jackson's thoughts were a whirlwind of Amelia's face and the future of the Montgomery Ranch. He knew he bore the hopes of not only Amelia's parents, but also the loyal ranch hands who depended on the land for their livelihoods. It was a heavy burden, yet one he willingly accepted. For Amelia, for the ranch, he would do whatever it took.

"Jackson," Amelia's father called out, his voice strained with worry. "Be careful out there."

"Of course, sir," Jackson replied, tipping his hat respectfully. "I'll do my best to find a resolution with the neighbors."

With a determined nod, Jackson urged his horse forward, leaving the familiar surroundings of the Montgomery Ranch behind. As he rode, he mulled over what he'd learned from Richard about the financial troubles plaguing the land. The low cattle prices and mounting debts were enough to dampen anyone's spirits, but he refused to let them extinguish the fire within him.

His first stop was the neighboring O'Sullivan Ranch, where the tension between the two families ran deep, fueled by accusations and mistrust. He dismounted outside the house, taking a moment to steel himself before knocking on the door.

"Mr. Turner," said Mr. O'Sullivan, his eyes narrowing suspiciously. "What brings you here?"

"Good evening, Mr. O'Sullivan," Jackson replied, forcing a polite smile. "I've come on behalf of Mr. Montgomery to discuss the ongoing dispute between your family and his. I believe it's time we found a resolution, for the sake of everyone involved."

"Is that so?" Mr. O'Sullivan crossed his arms, his grizzled face etched with doubt. "And what makes you think we'd be interested in anything you have to say?"

"I understand there's been bad blood between you and them," Jackson admitted, holding his ground. "But we must find a way to move forward, together. I'd like to offer my assistance as a third party to help find a solution. The ranches share this land and its resources, and if we don't work together, everyone will suffer the consequences."

"Consequences, huh?" Mr. O'Sullivan scoffed, yet there was a flicker of interest in his eyes.

"Yes," Jackson pressed on, sensing an opportunity. "We need to resolve this situation and find common ground, or else risk losing everything you've both worked so hard to build." He paused, measuring his words carefully. "What do you say, Mr. O'Sullivan? Can we at least try to settle our differences?"

Mr. O'Sullivan stared at him for a long moment, his expression hard to read. Then, finally, he nodded. "Alright. Let's talk."

As they stepped inside, Jackson knew this was only the beginning. But every journey began with a single step, and he was prepared to walk as far as necessary to save the Montgomery Ranch – and Amelia – from ruin.

***

Later that day, Jackson sat tall on his horse, flanked by the neighboring ranchers who had reluctantly agreed to meet with him. The tension in the air was palpable, like a coiled rattlesnake ready to strike.

"Alright," Jackson began, his voice steady despite the pounding of his heart. "We're all here because we share a common goal: the prosperity of our families and our ranches. I believe there's a way for us to achieve that without resorting to violence or underhanded tactics."

As he spoke, he couldn't help but think of Amelia's fiery spirit and determination. He knew she would have wanted him to bring peace to these neighbors, and it fueled his resolve.

"Listen," one of the ranchers, a burly man named Carson, cut in. "We ain't got nothin' against you personally, Turner, but the Montgomery's have been pushin' us around for too long. They've been encroachin' on our land, stealin' our cattle... We can't let 'em get away with it."

"Carson's right," another rancher, a wiry man named Bart, chimed in. "My family's worked this land for generations, just like the Montgomery's, and we won't be driven out by their greed."

Jackson raised a hand, stalling any further outbursts. "I understand your frustrations," he said, looking each of them in the eye. "But I also know that deep down, the Montgomery's care about this land and its people just as much as you do. They're not perfect, and neither are any of us. But I truly believe that if we work together, we can find a solution that benefits everyone."

He could see the skepticism in their eyes, but also a flicker of hope. They were desperate for change, and Jackson was determined to be the catalyst.

"Please," he implored, his voice softening with sincerity. "Give me a chance to make this right. For the sake of our families, our ranches, and the future of this land we all love so dearly."

There was a long pause, heavy with consideration. Finally, Carson broke the silence. "Alright, Turner. We'll give you a chance. But I swear, if the Montgomery's cross us again, there'll be hell to pay."

"Fair enough," Jackson agreed, nodding. "Thank you for your trust. I promise to do everything in my power to bring about a peaceful resolution."

For Amelia, for the Montgomery's, and for the future of this land, he could not falter.

A gust of wind picked up a cloud of dust, momentarily blocking the sun as it stretched long fingers across the parched landscape. Jackson squinted against the harsh light, his hat pulled low to shield his eyes. The ranchers' grievances echoed in his ears, each one a testament to the precarious balance they all walked in this unforgiving land.

"Jackson, we ain't asking for much, just a fair deal and some respect," Old Man Jenkins had said, his voice cracking with age and emotion. "But if the Montgomery's keep pushing us, we'll have no choice but to push back."

"Enough blood's been spilled on this soil," Jackson replied, his voice steady yet brimming with conviction. "I'll address your concerns with Mr. Montgomery, and together, we'll look for a way to restore peace to our community."

As the ranchers dispersed, each returning to their own homesteads, Jackson couldn't help but feel the weight of the responsibility he had just taken on. He knew the road ahead would be fraught with challenges and obstacles, but he was willing to face them head-on.

With a final nod, Jackson mounted his horse and set off for the Montgomery Ranch. His heart raced with determination, fueled by the trust placed upon him and the feelings he harbored for Amelia. As he rode, his thoughts were like tumbleweeds over the plains – the accusations of stolen cattle, the disputes over land boundaries, and the mounting debts threatening the very survival of the Montgomery Ranch.

He tightened his grip on the reins, guiding his horse through the familiar gates of the ranch. Amelia's father, a haggard figure draped in shadows, waited on the porch. Jackson dismounted, his boots crunching on the gravel as he approached.

"Mr. Montgomery," he began, his voice tinged with resolve. "I've spoken with the neighbors. They're frustrated and angry, but I believe there's still hope for a peaceful resolution. We must address their grievances, and I'm here to help you do that."

Amelia's father studied him for a moment, the lines on his face deepening with the weight of his worry. "Jackson, I don't know what we would do without you," he confessed, and there was a vulnerability in his voice that Jackson had never heard before. "These troubles are like a storm cloud hanging over our heads, and my Amelia is still missing..."

"Mr. Montgomery, I swear on everything I hold dear, I will do all within my power to protect this ranch, and to find Amelia," Jackson vowed, his gaze unwavering.

"Thank you, son," Amelia's father managed, gratitude thick in his voice. Then, with a sigh, he added, "Let's sit down and discuss what needs to be done. We'll find a solution."

As Jackson and Mr. Montgomery settled into rocking chairs on the porch, the creaking of their weight joined the symphony of crickets and rustling leaves, and it felt as if time itself had slowed. The tension in the air was palpable. Both men knew that the future of the ranch, and perhaps Amelia herself, hung in the balance.

"Jackson," Mr. Montgomery began, his voice rough with emotion, "I can't thank you enough for everything you've done so far. You've given us hope in a time when it seemed like all was lost."

"Well, this ranch is like a second home to me," Jackson replied, his eyes fixed on the horizon. "And Amelia... she's like family. I'd do anything to help make things right."

"Then let's put our heads together and figure something out," Mr. Montgomery sighed.

Jackson nodded, and the two men dove into a discussion of potential solutions. They weighed the pros and cons of securing a loan from the bank, knowing that it could be a difficult process. But without financial stability, they couldn't hope to resolve the disputes with their neighbors or focus on finding Amelia.

"Perhaps," Jackson suggested, "we could offer some sort of compromise to the neighboring ranchers. If we could reach an agreement about land usage and cattle grazing, maybe they'd be more willing to work with us."

"An interesting thought," Amelia's father mused, stroking his graying beard. "We've been at odds for so long, though. Do you really think they'd be open to negotiation?"

"From what I gathered during our conversations, it seems like they're just as tired of this conflict as we are," Jackson said, recalling the weariness in the ranchers' voices. "If we approach them with sincerity and a willingness to make concessions, I think they'll be receptive."

"Then, let's draw up a plan to propose to them." Amelia's father nodded decisively. "We'll also start looking into securing that loan. If we can solve both problems, it will give us the breathing room we need to focus on finding Amelia and putting our family back together," he said as they stood up and went inside.

The flickering lamplight danced in the dimly lit study, casting shadows on the walls as Jackson and Mr. Montgomery hunched over the weathered oak table. The weight of their conversation hung heavy in the air, but a spark of hope remained.

"Once we have the loan," Amelia's father said, tapping his fingers on the table's surface, "we'll be able to make some much-needed improvements to the ranch, and repair the fencing to mark the borders of our property. That should help us win back the trust of our neighbors and show them that we're willing to change."

"Agreed," Jackson replied, his jaw set with determination. He could see a future where the Montgomery Ranch thrived – a future that included finding Amelia and bringing her home safely.

"Jackson," Mr. Montgomery began, pausing as emotion choked his voice, "I can't express how grateful I am for everything you've done. You've given this family a fighting chance."

"Sir, there's no need to thank me," Jackson insisted, feeling a wave of warmth course through him despite the lingering chill in the room. "Amelia has been like a sister to me since we were children. I'd do anything to bring her back to you."

"Your loyalty and resourcefulness are a credit to your character, son," Mr. Montgomery said, clasping his hand firmly on Jackson's shoulder. "And I know Amelia would be proud of the man you've become."

As the words settled in his heart, Jackson felt an unwavering resolve take root within him. He knew that securing the loan and resolving the dispute with the neighboring ranchers was only part of the battle. But with each step forward, he was getting closer to finding Amelia.

"Tomorrow, we'll start making calls to secure the loan and schedule meetings with the neighboring ranchers," Jackson said resolutely. "We'll put this family back together. I promise you that."

"Thank you, Jackson," Amelia's father whispered, his eyes glistening with unshed tears. "I have faith in you."

Chapter 6: Uncovering the Past

The sun dipped low in the sky, casting a golden hue on the Montgomery Ranch. Jackson had spent the day poring over the family's belongings, searching for any clue that might lead him to his childhood friend.

The scent of aged leather and dust filled the air as he traced his fingers along the intricate wood carvings adorning the walls of the study. The room seemed frozen in time, untouched by the turmoil outside its doors. He could almost hear the laughter of better days echoing through the walls, and fondly ran his hand along them. Suddenly his fingertips brushed against a small indentation. Curiously, he pressed against it, feeling a hidden latch give way. A secret compartment revealed itself, nestled between the sprawling family portraits and shelves of dusty trinkets.

"What could this be?" Jackson whispered to himself. With great care, he pulled out a stack of old documents and faded photographs, feeling the weight of history in his hands.

"Maybe there's more to this than meets the eye," he murmured, settling into a worn leather armchair. He carefully examined each document, searching for any clues or connections to Samuel Caldwell – the man who had suddenly appeared in town around the time Amelia vanished.

Jackson sifted through yellowed letters, crinkling with age, and official-looking documents bearing the embossed seal of the Montgomery family. As he looked deeper into the past, he felt a growing sense of unease, like a cold wind whispering through the cracks in the walls.

"Samuel Caldwell... What could you possibly have to do with all this?" Jackson wondered aloud, his voice cracking with the strain of long hours spent sifting through the remnants of a family in turmoil.

"Amelia, wherever you are, I promise I won't stop until I find the truth," he vowed, his voice steady and resolute. With each document examined, the pieces of the puzzle drew closer together, forming a picture that would soon shatter the fragile truce between the past and present.

The air inside the hidden compartment grew colder as night crept in, and Jackson's breath fogged up the glass of a dusty picture frame. He lifted it up to catch the last rays of sunlight, revealing the faded photograph within. The image was old and frayed at the edges, but the subjects captured in time were unmistakable – Samuel Caldwell standing shoulder to shoulder with Amelia's parents, their smiles betraying an intimacy that sent a shiver down Jackson's spine.

"Well look at that..." Jackson muttered, his heart hammering against his ribs as the implications of the photograph took root in his mind. He traced his fingers over the familiar faces, noting the way Amelia's mother leaned into Samuel, her hand resting on his arm.

"Amelia... I've found something," he whispered to the empty room, as if she could hear him from the void she had vanished into. His resolve hardened, and determination blazed in his eyes like the fire of a thousand suns. "I'll confront Samuel and find out the truth about your disappearance, even if it means tearing this town apart."

As the night deepened, Jackson slipped the photograph into his pocket and made his way through the darkened halls of the Montgomery Ranch. Memories of simpler times spent with Amelia in these very rooms danced around him like ghosts, urging him forward, a lone beacon of hope in the darkness that threatened to swallow him whole.

"Samuel, you have no idea what you've unleashed," Jackson murmured, his voice tinged with steel as he stepped out into the moonlit night, the silver glow casting eerie shadows across the grounds.

"Your secrets won't stay hidden any longer, and I'll make sure the Montgomery family knows the depths of your treachery," he vowed, his heart pounding with a mix of fear and anticipation as he set off to confront the man who held the key to Amelia's fate.

With these words echoing in the darkness, Jackson rode towards the secluded cabin where Samuel Caldwell was known to reside. The rhythmic sound of hooves against the dusty earth provided a steady cadence as he approached his destination. An unsettling tension hung in the air, like a thunderstorm waiting to unleash its fury.

As the cabin came into view, it stood isolated from the world, shrouded by an eerie silence that seemed to echo the secrets hidden within. A flickering light from the window cast a warm glow onto the surrounding landscape, a deceptive beacon amidst the gathering darkness. With determination coursing through his veins, Jackson dismounted his horse and approached the cabin, each step leaving behind an imprint on the soft ground, charting his path towards the truth.

As he neared the cabin, the stillness was abruptly shattered by the sound of raised voices, their heated tones penetrating the thin wooden walls. He paused for a moment, listening intently to the unfolding argument, his heart pounding in anticipation of the confrontation that lay ahead.

"You think you can control everything, don't you Samuel?" a man snarled, anger dripping from every syllable. "But you've underestimated me, and I won't let your lies destroy anything else!"

Jackson's hand instinctively reached for the photograph tucked safely in his pocket, the image of Samuel with Amelia's parents serving as a reminder of the deceit that lay at the heart of the Montgomery family's suffering. His thoughts raced, wondering who could be confronting Samuel and what further treachery might be revealed.

"Who is this person? What might they know about Amelia?" Jackson pondered, his mind a whirlwind of questions and suspicions. He knew that he could not afford to wait any longer. The answers he sought were within his reach, and he would not allow Samuel's web of lies to ensnare the innocent any further.

"Amelia, I promised you justice," he murmured, his voice resolute with determination. "And tonight, I will keep that promise." With a renewed sense of purpose, Jackson steeled himself for the confrontation ahead, taking a deep breath as he prepared to enter the cabin and demand the truth from Samuel Caldwell.

The floorboards creaked beneath Jackson's boots as he cautiously stepped through the open front door, his gaze sweeping over the dimly lit cabin. Shadows danced upon the walls, cast by the flickering glow of the oil lamp that hung precariously from a nail on one of the wooden beams overhead. A thick layer of dust coated every surface, bearing testament to the secrets that had long festered within these four walls.

"Samuel, I don't want any part in this anymore!" the unknown man yelled, his voice shaking with anger, punctuating the charged air between them. The man stood with his back to Jackson, his identity obscured by the dim lighting.

Samuel's eyes flashed with anger, his fists clenched at his sides. "You're in too deep now," he growled, the menace in his tone unmistakable. "You can't back out."

"Can't I?" the stranger challenged, defiance seeping through his words.

Jackson's heart thundered in his chest, fueling the fire that roared within him - the fire that demanded justice for Amelia and her family. His mind raced, wondering if this mysterious person held the key to unraveling the twisted threads that bound Samuel Caldwell to the Montgomery's tragedy.

"Who is this man?" he wondered, his thoughts a storm of curiosity and determination. "Could he know where Amelia has been hidden? Or is he just another pawn in Samuel's twisted game?"

"Enough!" Jackson bellowed, unable to contain his fury any longer, his voice booming through the small cabin. "I've come for answers, Samuel, and you're going to give them to me!"

Both Samuel and the unknown man spun around, their faces turning pale as they registered Jackson's presence. Samuel's eyes widened in surprise, betraying the fear that gripped his soul as he realized that his secrets might finally be exposed.

"Jackson," Samuel stammered, his voice wavering as he fought to regain his composure. "I didn't expect you to... what are you doing here?"

"Looking for the truth," Jackson replied, his gaze never leaving Samuel's face. "The truth about your connection to the Montgomery family... and Amelia's disappearance."

"Yes!" the unknown man called out, his voice a mixture of relief and terror. "Samuel has-"

"Silence!" Samuel roared, cutting off the stranger's outburst with a vicious snarl. "This doesn't concern you!"

"Everything concerning Amelia concerns me," Jackson countered, his voice steady and resolute. "Now, tell me what's going on here, or so help me, I'll tear this place apart until I find the answers myself."

Samuel's gaze flickered between the stranger and Jackson, his face a mask of uncertainty that belied the storm of emotions within him. He swallowed hard, his Adam's apple bobbing as he struggled to marshal his thoughts and weigh the risks of exposing his secrets against those of defying Jackson's wrath.

"Alright," Samuel said finally, his voice low and defeated. "I'll tell you what you want to know."

"Good," Jackson replied, his eyes narrowing as he took a step closer to Samuel, his hands clenched into fists at his sides. "Start with how you're connected to Amelia and her family."

"Amelia's mother, Mary, was my sister," Samuel began hesitantly, his gaze darting to the floor as if in shame. "Years ago, I had a falling out with Mary and her husband over the ownership of the Montgomery Ranch. They thought they could cheat me out of my inheritance, my birthright." His voice trembled, anger dripping from every syllable. "They cast me aside like I was nothing, like I didn't even matter. So, I made it my mission to take back what was rightfully mine."

"Go on," Jackson urged, his heart pounding in his chest as he sensed that they were approaching the crux of the matter - the secret link between Samuel and Amelia's disappearance.

"Mary and I never made amends," Samuel continued, his voice growing hoarse as the weight of guilt and fear pressed down upon him. "When she died, I wanted revenge. Against those who had taken everything from me."

"Revenge?" Jackson echoed, his blood running cold as he began to piece together the fragments of Samuel's dark confession. "What does that have to do with Amelia?"

"Amelia..." Samuel trailed off, his eyes filled with a mixture of pain and regret. "Amelia was the key to it all. She was my one chance to reclaim what I'd lost - or so I thought."

"Explain," Jackson demanded, his voice taut with suspense and frustration. He could feel the truth beckoning to him, tantalizingly close yet still just out of reach.

"By making her disappear," Samuel whispered, his voice barely audible as he finally surrendered to the pressure of Jackson's relentless questioning. "I thought I could use her absence to manipulate the family, to turn them against one another and seize control of the ranch for myself."

"By orchestrating Amelia's disappearance?" Jackson asked, his voice laced with disgust. He watched as Samuel's eyes shimmered with unshed tears.

"Her disappearance provided the perfect opportunity for me to sow discord within the family," Samuel admitted, his voice barely audible above the crackling of the fire. "I never wanted to hurt her –

just manipulate the situation to my advantage. But things spiraled out of control, and now I don't know how to fix it."

Jackson clenched his fists in frustration, the nails digging into his palms as he struggled to maintain his composure. The man standing before him was revealed to be the very monster that had torn Amelia from her family and home. And all for the sake of revenge.

"Samuel," he growled, his voice cold and unforgiving. "You have to make this right. Tell me where Amelia is."

"Jackson, I..." Samuel hesitated, his gaze flickering between the floor and Jackson's furious eyes. "Please understand that I never meant for any of this to happen. But I'll do whatever it takes to make amends. Amelia...she's hidden away in an old warehouse in Pinesdale, a few miles from here."

"An old warehouse in Pinesdale?" Jackson repeated, his heart pounding in his chest as he pictured Amelia, alone and frightened in the darkness. "Is she safe? Is she even alive?"

Samuel swallowed hard, his face pale beneath the firelight. "As far as I know, yes. I made a deal with some folks.... Well, somehow things got out of hand...." He twisted his fingers nervously as he spoke.

The silence following Samuel's confession hung heavy in the air. Jackson clenched his fists, feeling tense as he fought to control the storm of emotions raging inside him. Anger and betrayal gnawed at his heart, threatening to consume him.

"Samuel," he said through gritted teeth, "you've betrayed not only Amelia but her entire family – your own blood. How could you?"

Samuel stared at the floor, shame etched into every line of his face. "It wasn't supposed to go this far, Jackson. I just wanted what was rightfully mine. But I let my desire for revenge cloud my judgment."

"Revenge?" Jackson scoffed. "What kind of man kidnaps his own niece for revenge? You've caused a lot of pain and suffering to those who trusted you!"

He paced across the cabin, the floorboards groaning beneath his boots. Every step was punctuated by the distant howling of the wind outside, as though nature itself mourned the loss of innocence within these walls.

"Jackson, please," Samuel pleaded, his eyes glistening with unshed tears. "I never intended to hurt her. I lost sight of what truly mattered – family, love, loyalty. My actions have brought me nothing but pain."

"Your pain is nothing compared to the anguish Amelia and her family have suffered!" Jackson snapped, his anger flaring anew. "You've destroyed lives, torn apart a family that once loved you. And for what? A piece of land? Your actions are unforgivable."

As the truth of Samuel's confession sank in, Jackson began to understand the depths of deceit and corruption that had festered within the Montgomery family. Power and greed had driven Samuel to commit a heinous act, breaking the bonds of love and trust that should have united them. This was a darkness that ran far deeper than he ever could have imagined.

"Jackson," Samuel whispered, broken by the weight of his sins, "I know I can never undo the harm I've caused."

"You better pray that she's alright. Because if anything happens to her, there will be nowhere you can hide from the consequences," said Jackson, swallowing the bitter taste of rage that still lingered at the back of his throat. He took a step towards the door.

With these words, Jackson turned his back on Samuel, striding toward the cabin door without sparing him another glance. As the cold wind whipped through the open doorway, he knew that he had no time to lose. He would find Amelia, bring her home, and somehow mend the shattered pieces of their lives together. No matter what it took, he would see justice done – for Amelia, her family, and himself.

Chapter 7: Chasing Shadows

As Jackson rode into Pinesdale on his trusty horse, dust swirled around him like a devilish dance, making it hard to see more than a few feet ahead. The town was a haphazard collection of buildings that seemed to have sprung up overnight – saloons, gambling dens, and boarding houses lined the streets, their faded signs creaking in the dry wind.

"Desperate men gather in desperate places," Jackson thought as he dismounted and scanned the scene before him. He led his horse to the nearest hitching post, giving her a reassuring pat on the neck before stepping onto the sidewalk. His boots echoed with each step, announcing his presence to anyone who might be watching.

"Amelia, I'll find you. I swear," he whispered under his breath, clutching the photo of her in his pocket. A familiar pang of longing and worry coursed through him as he remembered her delicate features and fiery spirit. She was always at the top of his mind, and although they were separated physically, he felt an intense mental connection with her.

He had never told Amelia how he felt about her. He wasn't totally sure himself what his feelings were, actually. He had never been in love and didn't know how to recognize it. But whatever he was feeling was stronger than friendship as it pulled him towards her, consuming his mind and heart.

He ducked into the nearest saloon, hoping to find someone who might have seen Amelia. The dimly lit establishment reeked of cigar smoke and stale whiskey, and a ragtime tune played on a battered piano in the corner. Jackson approached the bar, his eyes adjusting to the darkness as he surveyed the motley assortment of patrons nursing their drinks.

"Whiskey, please," he said, scanning the room for anyone who might have information. As the bartender slid a glass across the counter, Jackson leaned in and spoke in a low voice.

"Listen, I'm lookin' for someone. A young woman –" he pulled the photo from his pocket and held it up for the bartender to see. "Goes by the name Amelia Montgomery. She's got these distinctive green eyes, like emeralds, and hair as fiery as the desert sun."

The bartender studied the photo for a moment before shaking his head. "Can't say I've seen her, mister. But there's plenty of folks passin' through this town. You might want to ask around." He gestured vaguely toward the tables scattered throughout the saloon.

"Much obliged," Jackson said, nodding his appreciation. He took a sip of his whiskey, the burning liquid fortifying him for the task ahead. He knew he had to be discreet – Amelia's life could very well depend on it. With a steely determination, he moved from table to table, asking strangers about his missing friend while doing his best to blend into the rough crowd.

Through the haze of tobacco smoke and low murmurs, Jackson caught the eye of a man leaning against the far end of the bar, his gaze shrewd and calculating. The man's face was lined with age, a patchy beard peppered with gray framing his thin lips. He wore a simple apron over his clothes, signaling his role as the bar owner.

"Got a minute?" Jackson asked quietly, gesturing for the man to step into the shadows near the corner. The bar owner's eyes flicked down to the photo in Jackson's hand, then back up to meet his gaze. With a nod, he obliged, leading Jackson away from the crowded bar area.

"Word is you're lookin' for this Amelia Montgomery," the bar owner said, his voice hoarse and barely audible above the din of the saloon. "Might be I've seen her."

"Really?" Jackson's heart leaped at the prospect of a lead. He held out the photograph once more, careful not to let anyone else see it. "When?"

"Few days back, maybe a week," the man replied, scratching his unshaven chin. "Can't say for sure, but she had them green eyes like you mentioned. Fiery hair too."

"Where'd she go?" Jackson demanded, his pulse quickening as the possibility of finding Amelia grew nearer.

"Couldn't rightly say," the bar owner muttered, his gaze flickering past Jackson's shoulder toward a group of rough-looking men in the corner. They were huddled together, their laughter raucous and cruel. But as soon as they realized they were being watched, they fell silent, casting dark glances in their direction.

"Something wrong?" Jackson asked, noticing the sudden change in the room's atmosphere. The bar owner's eyes darted nervously between him and the men in the corner.

"Look, I can't help you no more," the man whispered urgently. "Just forget what I said, alright? You never heard a thing from me."

"Wait," Jackson urged, his grip on the photo tightening as suspicion twisted in his gut. "Why are you backing off now? What's going on?"

"Can't say nothin' more," the bar owner insisted, his voice trembling with fear. "You just keep your head down and get out of this town while you still can."

"What in the world," Jackson muttered, frustration coursing through him. He could feel the weight of the men's gazes on him, their eyes like vipers waiting to strike. The bar owner's sudden change of heart only deepened the mystery surrounding Amelia's disappearance.

Jackson kept his eyes trained on the group of rough-looking men as they left the bar, their laughter carrying on the dry wind. Amelia's face haunted his thoughts, her smile a beacon that guided him through the murky depths of this lawless town.

"Let's see where you're hiding your secrets," he muttered under his breath, adjusting the brim of his hat to conceal his face. He fell into step several paces behind the men, careful not to draw attention to himself.

"Hey, Pete," one of the men called out, slapping another on the back. "How 'bout that poker game last night? You still owe me twenty dollars!"

"Keep dreaming, Steve," the man named Pete retorted with a grin. "You know what they say about a fool and his money."

"Only fools I see are the ones who don't pay their debts," Steve shot back, laughter filling the air between them.

As the men bantered among themselves, Jackson couldn't help but wonder what part they played in Amelia's disappearance. Were they merely keeping an eye on him for someone else, or were they involved more deeply than he could imagine?

With each turn down the town's narrow streets, the buildings grew more dilapidated, their wooden frames warped by the relentless sun. The laughter of the men ahead seemed to echo off the rotting walls, mocking Jackson's quest. His boots kicked up clouds of dust as he trailed behind them, his senses sharpened in anticipation.

"Next time we see that stranger, we need to show him who's boss," Steve growled, the jovial tone gone from his voice. "Can't have no one pokin' around in our business."

"Right," Pete agreed. "We'll deal with him soon enough."

The outskirts of the town bled into a harsh, barren landscape, save for the crumbling warehouse that loomed ahead. Its walls were like the bones of a long-dead beast, bleached by the sun and left to erode under countless storms. Jackson peered at it from behind a withered cactus, his heart thudding against his ribs as he watched the group of outlaws approach the warehouse.

"Here we are," Bobby announced, pulling open the splintered door and allowing darkness to swallow them one by one. "Let's get down to business."

Jackson held his breath, waiting until their footsteps were swallowed by the foreboding interior before daring to move. He surveyed his surroundings, noting the way the wind seemed to whisper secrets through the desert brush. In that moment, he couldn't help but feel the weight of Amelia's absence pressing down on him, filling his chest with a painful longing.

With renewed determination, he crept forward, each step measured and deliberate as he neared the warehouse. He could hear the faint murmur of voices inside, punctuated by the occasional coarse laugh or thud of a table being struck. The rough edges of the worn wooden planks scraped against his fingertips as he pressed himself against the wall, straining to catch any mention of Amelia.

"Hey, you sure this is gonna work?" Pete asked, his words laced with doubt.

"Course it will," Bobby replied, confidence dripping from every syllable. "We got the girl, and Turner ain't got a clue what he's up against."

At the mention of Amelia, Jackson's pulse quickened, anger surging through his veins. He clenched his fists, nails digging into his palms as he fought the urge to burst through the door and confront them head-on. He knew that doing so would only put Amelia in greater danger, and he couldn't bear the thought of her suffering any more than she already had.

"Patience," he reminded himself, taking a deep breath to steady his nerves. "There's a time for action, and a time for strategy."

As his mind raced with the possibilities, Jackson vowed to keep a close watch on the warehouse, ready to seize any opportunity to rescue Amelia from her captors.

Jackson edged closer to the rickety warehouse door, his boots kicking up small puffs of dust with each deliberate step. The air was heavy with the scent of decay and neglect, a fitting backdrop for the nefarious deeds he suspected were unfolding within.

Pressing his eye to a narrow crack in the warped wood, Jackson strained to make out the figures huddled around a table in the dimly lit room. Their voices were a low murmur, punctuated by the occasional gruff laugh or sharp curse. The flickering glow of an oil lamp cast sinister shadows on their rough faces, each one marked with the lines of a life lived hard and fast.

"Time's runnin' short, boys," Dave, a wiry man with a crooked nose growled, his fingers drumming impatiently on the worn tabletop. "We gotta make our move soon, or we risk losin' everything."

"Easy for you to say," Pete retorted, his voice thick with resentment. "You ain't the one who's gonna have to face Turner when he comes lookin' for her."

"Relax, Pete," Steve sneered, leaning back in his chair with an air of satisfaction. "That boy don't stand a chance against us. He's as good as dead already."

Jackson knew that underestimating him would be their downfall.

As the outlaws continued their plotting, Jackson's thoughts raced like a wild stallion through the plains. If Amelia was indeed inside this warehouse, every second that passed increased the risk of her being harmed. He had to act swiftly and decisively enough to outwit the men who held her captive.

"Alright, boys," Bobby declared, slamming his fist on the table for emphasis. "Let's get down to business. Turner ain't gonna know what hit him."

"Neither will you," Jackson vowed silently, his eyes narrowing as he prepared to make his move. The time for strategy had come and gone. Now, it was a matter of heart - and he would lay his on the line for Amelia, come what may.

Jackson's gaze shifted from the outlaws to the interior of the warehouse. His heart pounded in his chest, but he willed himself to focus on the task at hand. He assessed the layout, noting the maze of crates stacked high, casting eerie shadows that danced with the flickering light. Several possibilities lay before him - a myriad of paths to Amelia, each fraught with danger and uncertainty.

"Think, Jackson," he muttered under his breath, his eyes scanning the room for any advantage. "There must be another way in."

As if in answer to his prayers, Jackson spotted a small door near the back of the warehouse, tucked away behind a pile of barrels. It was a discreet entry point, one that could allow him access without drawing too much attention. He knew it would be risky, but with Amelia's life on the line, there was no room for hesitation.

"Alright, boys," came Steve's gruff voice once more, jarring Jackson from his thoughts. "Let's hurry this up. We've got a lot of ground to cover tonight."

"Perfect," Jackson thought, his resolve steeling within him. "I need to act while they're preoccupied."

Taking a deep breath, he slunk back from his hiding spot and began to circle around the warehouse, keeping low to avoid detection. His boots crunched softly in the dust, the grit grinding between his teeth as he clenched his jaw with determination.

"Once I'm inside, I'll find Amelia and get her out," he told himself, his mind racing with plans. "But first, I need to deal with these outlaws."

The back entrance to the warehouse loomed before him, a weathered wooden door barely hanging onto its rusted hinges. As he reached for the handle, Jackson paused, his fingers hovering above the cold metal. This was the moment of truth, the point of no return.

With that thought, Jackson turned the handle and slipped through the door, his determination carrying him forward.

As he slipped inside, the dim glow of lantern light filtered through the cracks in the walls, barely illuminating the cavernous space. Shadows clung to every corner, their tendrils reaching out, threatening to ensnare him. He could hear the muffled voices of the outlaws nearby.

"Amelia must be here somewhere," he thought, his chest tightening with anxiety. "I've got to find her before they realize I'm here."

Moving deeper into the warehouse, Jackson scanned the area with hawk-like precision. His hands shook with a mixture of fear and anticipation, the weight of his revolver providing cold comfort.

He paused, listening intently as the outlaws' voices grew louder. They were close—too close for comfort. He could feel their malice seeping through the air like poison, suffocating him with its potency.

A bead of sweat trickled down Jackson's temple, but he dared not brush it away, lest the outlaws sense his presence. His pulse throbbed as he pressed himself against a stack of wooden crates. The musty scent of old leather and damp wood filled his nostrils.

"Boss says we gotta keep an eye on the girl," Dave grumbled, his voice as rough as gravel. "She's worth a pretty penny, that one."

"Damn right she is," Pete replied, a sinister chuckle lacing his words. "But I wouldn't mind having some fun with her."

Jackson clenched his fists, rage igniting within him like a wildfire. He pictured Amelia, her once vibrant spirit now surely dulled by fear and despair. How could this happen to her?

"Stay calm, Jackson," he thought, willing his heart to quiet its frenzied tempo. "You'll save her, but only if you keep your wits about you."

With deliberate precision, he edged around the crates and peered into the dimly lit space beyond. There they were, the outlaws sprawled around a makeshift table, their laughter a cruel mockery of camaraderie. Amelia was nowhere to be seen—yet he knew she had to be close.

"Showtime," he muttered under his breath, channeling every ounce of courage he possessed.

Stepping out from the shadows, Jackson leveled his revolver at the group, each man's face a portrait of shock and disbelief.

"Evenin', gentlemen," he drawled, his voice a deadly purr. "The lady you're holdin' captive—I suggest you release her. Now."

"Who do you think you are?" Pete demanded, his hand inching towards his own weapon.

"Doesn't matter who I am," Jackson replied, a fierce glint in his eyes. "What matters is that you're standin' between me and Amelia, and I don't take kindly to that."

"Amelia?" Dave sneered, the name dripping with disdain. "So, you're the one she's been whining for all this time. Well, ain't that sweet?"

"Enough talk," Jackson growled, his finger tightening on the trigger. "Bring her out now, or I'll shoot every last one of you."

"Alright, alright," Bobby, the leader of the group conceded, raising his hands in surrender. "No need for bloodshed. We'll get your girl, but just remember—this ain't over."

"Wouldn't dream of it," Jackson retorted, his expression steely as he kept his gun trained on the outlaws.

"Here she is," Pete grunted, pulling a disheveled, trembling Amelia into the open.

"Jackson," she whispered, tears streaming down her face. "I knew you'd come for me."

"Of course," Jackson replied tenderly, his heart swelling at the sight of her.

"Alright, lover boy," Bobby taunted, a wicked grin splitting his face as he held a gun to Amelia's head. "You got to see your girl. Now, let's see if you can make it out alive."

And with that, the warehouse erupted into chaos, leaving Jackson and Amelia to fight their way through a storm of bullets and betrayal—a desperate battle whose outcome was far from certain.

Chapter 8: Facing Danger

Jackson had been warned about this place - the foreboding chasm known as Devil's Hideout with its razor-sharp rocks and deadly pitfalls - but nothing could have prepared him for the real thing. He had followed the outlaws after two of them had grabbed Amelia and fled during the shootout. With each step, the shadows of the canyon walls grew darker, swallowing him whole into their treacherous embrace.

As Jackson entered the canyon, he felt as though he was stepping into a different world. The air was cooler here, damp and heavy with an unspoken threat. His heart pounded in his chest, anticipation and fear warring for dominance in the recesses of his mind. Every sense was on high alert, attuned to the slightest whisper of danger.

"Stay focused, Turner," he muttered under his breath, trying to calm his racing thoughts. "You've faced worse than this."

Eyes scanning the rugged terrain, Jackson moved cautiously, placing each foot deliberately on the loose gravel beneath him. His boots crunched and slid, the sound echoing like thunder off the canyon walls. Every shift in the wind, every creak of tortured rock set his pulse pounding anew, a reminder of the danger lurking behind every shadow.

"Focus," Jackson reminded himself once more, pushing aside the distraction and fixing his gaze on the path ahead. For now, the only thing that mattered was putting one foot in front of the other, navigating the treacherous terrain step by precarious step.

A sudden gust of wind snaked through the canyon, stirring up a cloud of dust that swirled around him like an otherworldly specter. He squinted against the stinging grit, and in that fleeting moment of impaired vision, he saw it – a flicker of movement up ahead.

"Amelia," he breathed, his heart seizing with a jolt of hope and dread. Through narrowed eyes, he discerned the figures of the outlaws who held her captive. They were mere shadows themselves, blending into the canyon's shadows with sinister ease.

"Let her go!" Jackson roared, the sound echoing off the canyon walls. He knew it was a foolish move, revealing his presence, but the sight of Amelia – her beautiful face streaked with dirt and fear – ignited something primal within him.

"Jackson?" Amelia's voice wavered, nearly drowned by the howling wind. Her captor tightened his grip on her arm, causing her to wince in pain. "Please, don't hurt him!" she begged the man.

"Keep quiet, girl!" Bobby snarled, pressing the cold barrel of his revolver against her temple. "Or I'll make you regret it."

"Over my dead body," Jackson muttered under his breath, adrenaline coursing through his veins. As if propelled by an unseen force, he broke into a sprint, determined to reach Amelia before the outlaws could inflict more harm.

"Jackson, no!" Amelia cried out, panic lacing her words. But he wouldn't be deterred. He'd faced down countless dangers in his life, and these outlaws were no different. He knew their kind – ruthless, greedy men who preyed upon the innocent.

"Stop him!" Pete barked, his voice a venomous snarl. Shots rang out, but Jackson didn't falter. The canyon walls seemed to close in around him, narrowing his focus until all that remained was Amelia's terrified gaze, beckoning him onward.

The wind whipped through Jackson's hair as he raced toward the outlaws, Amelia's anguished cries still ringing in his ears. The canyon grew treacherous, its twisted pathways narrowing into gauntlets of jagged rock. As the chase intensified, Jackson's breaths came in gasps, his muscles burning with exertion.

"Give it up, Turner!" Bobby shouted, taking a wild shot that ricocheted off the canyon wall, mere inches from Jackson's head. "You ain't gonna save her!"

"Amelia's worth more than you'll ever be," Jackson spat back, his voice hoarse and raw with determination.

"Jackson, be careful!" Amelia cried, her voice strained with desperation.

"Keep your pretty little mouth shut!" Pete snapped, yanking her roughly by the arm as they continued walking.

"Touch her again and I'll make you regret it!" Jackson roared, fueled by both love and fury. His heart hammered in his chest, blood thundering in his ears, drowning out all other sounds save for the pounding of boots against the unforgiving earth.

Inwardly, he cursed himself for not having been there to protect Amelia sooner. He knew what it meant to lose someone – the aching emptiness, the hollow ghost of memories haunting every waking moment. And he couldn't bear the thought of losing her too.

As the distance between them began to close, Jackson willed every ounce of strength he had into his legs, pushing himself harder than ever before. He knew the odds were stacked against him – two gunslingers and a canyon full of danger. But he was never one to back down from a challenge.

"Jackson!" Amelia called out, hope blossoming in her voice as she saw him drawing near.

"Almost there," he assured her, his breaths ragged and labored, his muscles screaming in protest. But he wouldn't give up, not while Amelia was still in danger. And as he vaulted over one last rocky obstacle, his eyes locked onto hers for a moment.

The wind howled through the canyon, stirring up clouds of dust as it whipped past Jackson's face. He could feel his heart thudding against his ribs, his every breath a painful gasp as he raced after the outlaws and their captive.

"Jackson!" Amelia cried out, her voice echoing off the shadowy canyon walls. She was so close now – but with those two outlaws at her side, she might as well have been a thousand miles away.

"Wait a minute," he thought, a sudden idea taking shape in his mind as he quickly darted to the side. "What if I can use these shadows to my advantage..."

"Hey!" Bobby shouted, noticing Jackson's sudden change in tactics. "Where do you think you're goin'?"

"Getting real tired of you boys," Jackson called back, his voice laced with heavy sarcasm as he ducked behind a large boulder. "Thought I'd give you a chance to catch your breath."

"Get back here, you coward!" Pete snarled, firing off a wild shot in Jackson's direction. The bullet ricocheted off the rock, sending a shower of sparks into the air.

"Aw, now you've gone and hurt my feelings," Jackson taunted, the corner of his mouth quirking up into a dangerous grin. "But since you asked so nicely..."

In one swift movement, he sprang from behind the boulder, his boots skidding on the loose gravel as he closed the distance between them. The outlaws' eyes widened in surprise, their fingers twitching toward their holsters – but Jackson was already one step ahead.

"Y'all have no idea who you're messin' with," Jackson said, his voice low and dangerous.

"Seems to me like we're the ones holdin' all the cards here, boy," Bobby drawled, casting a sidelong glance at Amelia. She stood beside him, her face streaked with dust and sweat, but her chin held high in defiance.

Jackson's heart clenched at the sight of her, and he tightened his grip on his gun. "You touch one hair on her head, and I swear I'll make you regret it."

"Big words for a man outnumbered," sneered Pete, his laughter grating and cruel. But as the echoes of his mirth bounced off the canyon walls, Jackson noticed something – a faint tremor in the man's hand, the way his gaze darted nervously between Jackson and Amelia.

His mind raced, thoughts flying faster than the bullets he'd fired in countless duels before. These men were brutes, yes, but they were also human, and humans could be frightened, manipulated, outwitted. If he played his cards right, perhaps he could turn this situation to his advantage.

"Outnumbered, sure," Jackson replied, his tone deceptively casual. "But let me ask you something – how many guns does it take to kill a man?"

Before the outlaws had a chance to respond, Jackson lunged to the side, his boots skidding across the loose gravel as he scrambled for cover behind a nearby boulder. The outlaws shouted in surprise, their weapons drawn and ready, but Jackson was already calculating his next move.

"Get him!" Bobby roared, his face twisted with rage as he gestured towards Jackson's hiding spot.

Jackson's heart pounded like a drum in his chest, his breath coming in ragged gasps as he peered around the edge of the boulder. He could see Amelia, her eyes wide with terror but also filled with determination, silently urging him to act.

"Come on out, boy!" Pete taunted, his revolver cocked and aimed at the boulder. "Your little game ain't foolin' anyone!"

"Alright," Jackson whispered under his breath, steeling himself for what was to come. "Let's give 'em a show."

In that instant, Jackson sprang from his hiding spot, his gun raised and his finger poised on the trigger. As the outlaws turned towards him in surprise, he fired off a rapid series of shots, echoing through the canyon like a symphony of chaos and destruction.

Jackson's hand hovered above his holster, his fingers twitching with anticipation. His eyes were locked with Bobby, the outlaw leader, as each waited for the other to make a move.

"Looks like we got ourselves a good ol' fashioned standoff here," Bobby sneered, his voice dripping with malice. "You think you're fast enough to take us on, boy?"

"Guess we'll just have to find out," Jackson replied coolly, his gaze never wavering from the man's cold eyes. Amelia watched their exchange with bated breath, her chest heaving with silent sobs.

"Last chance, boy," Bobby growled. "Walk away now, and maybe we'll let the girl live."

"Let her go first," Jackson countered, his voice steady despite the adrenaline coursing through his veins. "Then I'll leave."

"Ha! You ain't in no position to be making demands!" Bobby spat, but Jackson could see the flicker of doubt in his eyes.

In that split second, as Bobby hesitated, Jackson seized his opportunity. He drew his gun with lightning speed, taking aim at the man. The shot rang out, echoing through the canyon like a vengeful roar.

"Amelia, get down!" Jackson shouted, his voice laced with urgency. The terrified woman didn't need to be told twice as she dropped to the ground just as the outlaws opened fire.

"We'll get you, Turner!" Bobby cried, unleashing a hail of bullets in Jackson's direction. But Jackson was already moving, diving behind a large rock as he returned fire with skilled accuracy.

"Thought you could outsmart us, huh?" Pete mocked, his voice barely audible over the gunfire. "You ain't nothin' but a dead man now!"

"Your mistake was underestimating me," Jackson thought grimly, gritting his teeth as he quickly assessed his situation. With each passing second, the odds seemed to be stacking up against him – but there was no way he was going to let Amelia down.

"Time to end this," he muttered to himself. With one final, deep breath, Jackson steeled himself for what could very well be his last stand.

***

With the canyon engulfed in a haze of smoke and dust, and the scent of gunpowder lingering heavily in the air, Jackson pressed on. The rapid pounding of his heart echoed the rhythm of gunfire that had finally ceased, replaced by an eerie silence. His fingers tightened around the grip of his revolver, its barrel still searing hot from the relentless exchange of shots. He scanned the rocky terrain, taking in the prone forms of the outlaws sprawled across the ground, their lifeless eyes staring at nothing.

"Amelia," he breathed, her name a whispered prayer upon his lips. It was as if time slowed, each step towards her dragging on for an eternity. Finally, he reached Amelia's side, where she huddled behind a boulder, eyes wide with terror but alive.

"Jackson!" she choked out, throwing herself into his arms with abandon. Relief surged through him like a tidal wave, drowning out the pain and exhaustion that had threatened to overwhelm him just moments before.

"Amelia, I've got you now." He held her tightly, feeling the tremors running through her body gradually subside. "You're safe."

"Jackson, you... you saved me." She gazed up at him, her eyes shimmering with unshed tears. "I don't know how I can ever repay you."

"Seeing you safe is all the payment I need," he murmured, his voice thick with emotion. As they stood locked in their embrace, the vastness of the canyon seemed to shrink away, leaving only the two of them and the overwhelming connection forged through shared danger and devotion.

"Where do we go from here?" Amelia asked, her voice barely audible as it was carried away on the breeze that whispered through the canyon.

"First things first, we need to get out of this place," Jackson answered, his thoughts already racing ahead to their next move. He knew that danger could be lurking in the shadows.

"Let's get you home, Amelia," he said with determination, guiding her away from the scene of carnage and towards the promise of safety. For Jackson, there was no greater treasure than the woman in his arms.

Chapter 9: Closure

"Amelia," Jackson breathed, standing beside her, and enveloping her in his strong arms. "You're safe."

"Thank you," Amelia sobbed into his chest, clinging to him as if he were her lifeline. "I didn't know how much longer I could go on like this."

"Shhh, it's over now," Jackson murmured, stroking her hair.

Together, they had finally reached the Montgomery ranch. A knock upon the door brought Mr. and Mrs. Montgomery rushing forward as Amelia stepped into view.

"My sweet girl!" cried Mrs. Montgomery, tears streaming down her face as she enveloped Amelia in a warm embrace.

"Thank you, Jackson," Mr. Montgomery choked out, visibly shaken as he wiped tears from his eyes. "You've brought our daughter back to us."

"Welcome home, sis," said Amelia's brother Robert, his voice wavering with emotion.

As the family embraced, tears of relief mingling with the dust on their cheeks, Jackson stepped back and took a moment to let it all sink in. He had done it – he had unraveled Amelia's mystery and returned her safely to her loved ones. But more than that, he had proven to himself that he was capable of accomplishing great things and protecting those he cared about.

"Jackson," Amelia said, breaking away from her family and turning to face him. "I can never repay you for all you've done."

"Your safety is all the payment I need," Jackson replied, his eyes meeting hers with a depth of understanding forged by shared history and their recent ordeal. "But I think we have some catching up to do, don't we?"

"Indeed we do," Amelia agreed with a smile.

Jackson closed his eyes briefly, allowing himself to reflect on the arduous journey that had brought him to this point. He recalled the first desperate pleas from the Montgomery family when they sought his help in finding Amelia, the countless sleepless nights spent piecing together the puzzle to locate her, and the grueling battles against both man and nature along the way.

His heart swelled with pride as he acknowledged the growth he had experienced throughout the adventure. He had faced challenges that would have broken lesser men, yet he had emerged stronger and more confident in himself and his abilities. He had learned to trust his instincts and fight for what he believed in, even when the odds seemed insurmountable.

"Your tenacity is inspiring, Jackson," Amelia's father said, his voice thick with emotion. "You've shown us all what true courage and determination look like."

"Thank you," Jackson replied, his gaze drifting towards Amelia. "But I couldn't have done it without the support of everyone here. We all played a part in this journey."

"Still," Amelia interjected, her eyes shimmering with unshed tears, "it was your unwavering determination that led us to this moment. You're the reason we can finally start to heal."

"Amelia's right," Robert chimed in, his voice steady and sincere. "We owe you our deepest gratitude, Jackson."

"Happy to help," Jackson said softly.

***

In the fading light of day, Jackson stood at the edge of the Montgomery Ranch, watching as the sun dipped below the horizon. The sky was set ablaze with a symphony of colors, painting the land in shades of gold and crimson – a fitting backdrop for the emotional journey they had all just weathered. He took a deep breath, inhaling the scent of sagebrush that mingled with the crisp evening air, grounding himself in the reality of Amelia's safe return.

"Jackson," Amelia called softly as she approached him, her voice a gentle melody carried on the breeze. He turned to face her, his eyes roaming over her features before resting on the tender smile gracing her lips. She had taken a shower and changed into a clean dress and looked quite beautiful. He could smell the fragrant aroma of her freshly washed auburn hair as she stood close to him, looking up with shimmering green eyes.

"Amelia, I..." he began, struggling to find the right words amidst the whirlwind of emotions threatening to overwhelm him. He wanted to tell her how he felt. He wanted to kiss her and hold her and never let her go.

But what if she didn't feel the same way? And was he ready to give up his rambling cowboy lifestyle to settle down? It was all he'd ever known. It was who he was. Deep down, in his blood he was a cowboy. But was it all he would ever be? The thoughts pounded in his head as he remained at a loss for words. Before he could say anything, Mrs. Montgomery appeared at Amelia's side, placing a hand on her daughter's shoulder.

"Jackson," she said, her voice laden with gratitude, "we can never repay you for what you have done for our family. Your courage and unwavering determination brought Amelia back to us."

"Yes," Amelia beamed happily, her beautiful green eyes shining with admiration, "Jackson, you're my hero," she blushed as she said the words, smiling at him.

As the weight of their words settled, Jackson felt a sense of longing wash over him. "There's nothing that would've stopped me from bringing you back safely, Amelia," he said as he looked deep into her eyes.

"Then let this not be a farewell, but a promise to return," Mrs. Montgomery said, extending her hand. "Our door will always be open to you, Jackson."

"Thank you," Jackson murmured, clasping her hand in a firm grip. Then he turned to Amelia, the lingering embers of their shared history igniting something within him.

"Amelia," he whispered, leaning in close so that only she could hear, "Know that I will carry our memories with me forever."

***

The sun dipped low in the sky, casting a warm glow over the Montgomery Ranch. Shadows danced playfully across the freshly mended fences and walls, as if nature itself recognized that the darkness which had once engulfed this place was now banished. The air hummed with an atmosphere of closure and relief, each breath drawn by those who lived and worked here filled with newfound tranquility.

In the courtyard, laughter rang out and the birds sang happily. The Montgomery family had gathered with friends to celebrate Amelia's return. The weight of fear and uncertainty that had pressed down upon them for so long was finally lifted, and the joy in their hearts could not be contained.

"Can't remember the last time we had us a proper celebration 'round these parts," said Bill, the ranch hand, his weathered face creasing into a wide grin as he clapped Robert on the back.

"Neither can I," replied Robert, his eyes shining with happiness and gratitude as he looked around at his sister and their reunited family. "But there's no better reason than Amelia's safe return."

As the feast began, with tables full of delicious home-cooked food, Jackson found himself sitting beside Amelia. They shared knowing glances and soft smiles, their bond forged in their recent experiences. The connection they felt was undeniable, yet tempered by the knowledge that Jackson's cowboy spirit beckoned him towards new horizons.

"Jackson," Amelia whispered, her voice barely audible over the revelry, "I just wanted you to know how much it means to all of us that you never gave up. It feels like a lifetime ago that I lost my way, but you risked everything to rescue me."

"Amelia, it was my honor," Jackson responded quietly, his fingers brushing against hers. "Your courage and strength inspired me every step of the way. I'm just glad I could help you find your way back to your family."

"Sometimes I think the darkness we face changes us," Amelia said, her gaze flickering briefly towards the setting sun. "But seeing everyone here, together, makes me believe that perhaps we can heal in time."

"Scars may remain, but they are a testament to our resilience," Jackson mused. "And in facing that darkness, we've learned the true value of the light."

Emboldened by his words and the spirit of hope that filled the air, Amelia leaned in closer, her voice soft but steady. "I'll never forget the part of my life that you saved, Jackson. And though you may roam far and wide, know that you will always have a place here."

"Thank you, Amelia," Jackson whispered, their fingers intertwining for a fleeting moment. "That means more to me than words can express."

"Promise me," Amelia whispered, her eyes glistening with unshed tears. "Promise me that no matter what happens, we'll always find our way back to each other."

"Always," he vowed, sealing the promise with a gentle kiss on her cheek.

As the sun sank beneath the horizon, the sky ablaze with the colors of twilight, the Montgomery Ranch—a once fractured family now whole again—embraced the promise of a brighter future. And as Jackson's heart swelled with the love and gratitude of those he had helped, he knew that no matter where his journey took him, the memories forged here would be carried with him always.

The following morning, the sun crept over the horizon, casting a warm golden light across the fields of the Montgomery Ranch. It was as if the land itself had been reborn, mirroring the newfound hope that blossomed within the hearts of its inhabitants. As Amelia and her family stood together on the porch, they shared their dreams for the future—their plans to rebuild the ranch into something stronger than before.

"Imagine it, Amelia," her father said, his eyes shining. "A new beginning for our family, here on this land we've fought to protect."

"Yes," she agreed, her gaze sweeping over the vibrant pastures, ripe with possibility. "We've got a lot of work ahead of us, but I believe we can make our ranch prosper again."

All around them, the community had gathered in support—neighbors who had banded together through Jackson's peacemaking efforts. They offered their help with the ranch, each eager to repay Jackson for his fearless dedication in bringing Amelia back home.

"Jackson," called out Old Man Jenkins, the town blacksmith, as he approached with a firm handshake. "You've done right by this family and by all of us. We're proud to know you and stand beside you."

"Thank you," Jackson said, offering a humble nod. But within him, he could not ignore the swell of pride that came from knowing he had made a positive impact on people's lives.

"Your courage is unmatched, son," chimed in Mr. O'Sullivan. "You're a true hero to us all."

"I appreciate that," Jackson replied, his cheeks reddening beneath the weight of such praise. In his heart, he knew that it wasn't heroism that had driven him forward, but the unwavering love he held for Amelia and her family. Still, the recognition from those around him was a testament to the difference one man could make.

As the sun climbed higher in the sky, casting long shadows across the bustling ranch, Jackson couldn't help but feel a deep sense of satisfaction. In solving the mystery of Amelia's disappearance, he had not only saved her life but also unearthed a newfound purpose within himself. And as he stood there among the smiling faces of the community, basking in the warmth of their gratitude, Jackson knew that his journey was far from over. The wide-open frontier beckoned, filled with unknown challenges and countless opportunities to continue making a difference in this wild, beautiful world.

"Jackson," Amelia whispered, her fingers brushing against his, "Thank you for everything."

"Amelia," he replied softly, meeting her eyes, "It was always my pleasure."

The sun dipped low in the sky, casting a golden hue over the Montgomery Ranch. Jackson stood near his trusty horse, his heart heavy with both joy and sorrow. The time had come to say goodbye.

"Mr. Montgomery," Jackson said, extending his hand to Amelia's father.

"Jackson," Mr. Montgomery replied, gripping his hand firmly, "You've done more for our family than we could have ever asked for. You're always welcome here."

"Thank you," Jackson nodded.

He then turned to Amelia's mother, Mrs. Montgomery, who embraced him tightly. "Promise me you'll keep in touch, Jackson," she whispered, her voice thick with emotion.

"I promise," he assured her.

"Amelia," Jackson began, turning to face the woman who had captured his heart all those years ago. Her eyes glistened with unshed tears as she smiled at him, a look of adoration in her eyes.

"Jackson," Amelia replied, her voice barely above a whisper. "You know how much I appreciate you—how much we all do."

"Amelia," Jackson murmured, his hand instinctively reaching for hers, "Knowing that means more to me than you can imagine."

"Take care of yourself out there," Amelia said gently, squeezing his hand one last time before finally releasing it.

With a bittersweet smile, Jackson tipped his hat to the gathered members of the Montgomery family. "Until we meet again."

Climbing onto his horse, he looked up at the ranch. The sun's last rays danced upon the vibrant green grass, and a gentle breeze rustled the leaves of the old oak tree near the house.

As he rode away, the sun dipped below the horizon, painting the sky with fiery shades of orange and red. The world around him seemed to be urging him onwards towards new adventures.

With each hoofbeat echoing in his ears, Jackson felt a wave of fulfillment wash over him. He had brought Amelia home, reunited a family, and found justice for those who had sought to harm them. And though it was hard to leave behind the people who were like family to him, he knew that his purpose lay out there on the frontier.

***

As the dust settled on the small town, Jackson found himself at a crossroads. The call of the open range echoed in his restless soul, and the nomadic spirit that had driven him across the rugged landscapes seemed to pull him away once more.

However, amidst the sagebrush and tumbleweeds, he felt himself torn between the allure of the untamed wilderness and the warm embrace of the woman he loved. Her eyes held the promise of a settled life, a quiet homestead, and an anchor in a world of chaos. Yet, the lonesome wind carried the haunting whispers of adventure, sparking the embers of a yearning that refused to be extinguished.

Jackson grappled with the tension between the untamed calling of his heart and the grounded roots he could plant with Amelia, standing at the threshold of a choice that would define the path of his wandering spirit.

"Goodbye, Amelia," he whispered to the wind as he rode off into the sunset, the promise of future adventures calling to him like a siren's song.

The vast expanse of the wild west stretched out before Jackson as he rode on, his horse's hooves pounding a steady rhythm beneath him. The dry air carried the scent of sagebrush and dust, while the distant mountains stood tall against the deepening blue sky. It was a landscape that had always felt like home to him, and now, with the resolution of the Montgomery case behind him, it felt even more so.

"Never thought I'd see the day where I'd be ridin' off into the sunset after savin' a damsel in distress," Jackson thought aloud, a hint of amusement in his voice. His trusty horse snorted in response, flicking an ear back towards him. "What do you think, Butterscotch? You reckon we got what it takes to be heroes?"

As he continued riding, Jackson mulled over the lessons he had learned during the investigation. He had faced adversity, deceit, and danger head-on, discovering reserves of strength and courage within himself that he hadn't known existed. He had also witnessed the power of love and loyalty to bind people together, even in the darkest of times.

"Amelia and her family... they taught me somethin' important," he murmured, his eyes fixed on the disappearing sun. "They showed me that there's more to life than just chasin' down outlaws and findin' stolen cattle. There's love, friendship, and trust too."

Butterscotch shook her mane, snapping Jackson from his reverie. He realized then that his newfound skills could make a real difference in the world. There were countless stories of heartache and injustice waiting to be righted, and he could be the one doing the righting. The mere thought of it sent a thrill coursing through his veins.

"Alright, Butterscotch," he declared with determination, his voice carrying on the wind. "We've got us a new mission now. We're gonna keep fightin' for justice, for the folks who can't fight for themselves."

The horse whinnied in agreement, as if understanding the gravity of the words spoken. Together, they rode through the wild west, with a renewed purpose and a fire ignited within their hearts.

"Who knows," Jackson said, his voice tinged with excitement. "Maybe one day, we'll even find ourselves ready to settle down. But until then, we've got plenty of work to do."

The sun dipped low in the sky, casting fiery hues across the horizon as Jackson and Butterscotch made their way along a dusty trail. The landscape stretched out before them, with mountains towering in the distance and the desert blooming with vibrant cacti. It was a world full of danger and beauty, a place where both love and heartache could leave their marks.

"Y'know, girl," Jackson mused aloud, his eyes scanning the horizon for any sign of trouble. "I reckon we're gonna see a whole lot more of this wild land before we're through. Seems like there's always somethin' goin' on out here," he said, his voice filled with both excitement and wonder.

As they rode, Jackson contemplated the many adventures that lay ahead of him. He imagined the people he would meet, the lives he would change for the better, and the mysteries he would unravel. And though he didn't know precisely what awaited him, he felt anticipation flowing through his veins like an untamed stallion.

"Alright then, partner," Jackson said, his voice filled with determination. "Let's see what this wild west has in store for us."

With that, Jackson spurred Butterscotch into a faster gallop, the two of them disappearing into the golden horizon, ready to face whatever challenges lay ahead. The world was wide open before him, waiting to be explored.

Chapter 10: New Beginnings

In the weeks that followed, Jackson tried to enjoy the carefree cowboy life he'd always lived, roaming the untamed frontier, but something was different. His heart yearned for Amelia and the promise of what could be. He'd always known that it would take a remarkable woman to tame his wild soul. Maybe she was the one.

"Is this the end of our story, Amelia?" he wondered, his heart aching at the thought. "No, I won't let it be."

As he rode through the rugged terrain, the memory of Amelia lingered in his thoughts like the sweet scent of wildflowers. The realization hit him like a sudden storm on the horizon – he loved her more than the call of the open range. His heart, once restless and free, now yearned for the warmth of her touch, her soft embrace, and the tender smile that only Amelia could bring.

With a determined gleam in his eyes, Jackson spurred his horse toward the Montgomery Ranch, flooded by the storm of emotions that raged within him. As he approached the homestead, the distant noise of cattle mingled with the soft whisper of the wind through the grass.

He stopped his horse at the edge of the fence and dismounted, suddenly overwhelmed with what was happening. Was he really about to give up his cowboy ways? Was he ready to settle down and start a new life? The thoughts tore his mind apart as he stood there next to Butterscotch debating whether to walk toward the ranch or ride off into the sunset.

The door suddenly swung open, and there she stood, framed in the warm glow of the setting sun. Their eyes met, and in that moment, words became unnecessary.

Jackson ran towards her, closing the gap between them, and lifted Amelia up into his strong arms as they kissed passionately. In the embrace of that quiet evening, under the endless canvas of the Montana sky, Jackson realized that the greatest adventure he sought had been right here all along – in the love he found with Amelia. The winds of change had settled, and he had returned home, not to the frontier's call, but to the embrace of the woman who had captured his wandering heart.

"Is it really you?" Amelia whispered, her voice muffled by his shirt, after they finished their long kiss mingled with laughter and tears.

"Yes, it's me," he assured her, pressing his lips tenderly to the top of her head. "I realized I couldn't live without you."

"I thought you'd never come back," she cried, unable to stop the tears from falling. "When you left, you took my heart with you. I waited for you every day, hoping you'd return."

Jackson felt the tears in his eyes as he held her close. "Amelia, I've fallen hard for you. I tried to deny it. I thought I could go back to the wild west like before, but it wasn't the same. When I rescued you, I hadn't realized my true feelings. But after I left, my heart wouldn't let me stay away from you any longer."

Amelia wept with pure joy at hearing his words. "My heart has belonged to you since we were kids, Jackson Turner. But I realized you'd have to be the one to choose me over the open range. I could never hold you back from it," she blushed. "I always wanted you to be my cowboy."

***

The sun shone brightly in the sky, casting a golden hue across the Montgomery Ranch. Jackson stood at the edge of the corral, the warm wood beneath his fingers as he watched Amelia tending to her favorite mare, Sundance, with gentle hands. The sight of her laughter and the way her beautiful auburn hair blew in the breeze filled him with an abiding sense of peace.

It had been several weeks since Jackson had returned to the ranch. The Montgomery family had gotten the loan and things had already started to improve financially. Jackson had been hired as a ranch hand, and he was really enjoying the stability of life there.

"Y'know, Jackson," drawled Robert, leaning against a nearby fence post, "I reckon there's more to life than chasin' after outlaws and fightin' off danger."

"True enough," Jackson replied, a thoughtful smile tugging at the corners of his mouth. He couldn't help but agree. As his gaze lingered on Amelia, he considered the lessons learned – trust, loyalty, and the strength born of love.

"Amelia and I, we've been through a lot," he mused aloud, looking at her brother. "But it's made us stronger, closer. It's taught me that when you love someone, you fight for them, no matter the odds."

Robert nodded in agreement, his eyes reflecting the wisdom of a man who'd seen his share of hardship. "That's right, partner. And sometimes, it's the journey itself that makes us who we are."

"Speaking of journeys," Jackson said, his eyes never leaving Amelia, "I can't wait to see where life takes us next."

"Jackson!" Amelia called, her voice lilting on the breeze. She beckoned him over, her cheeks flushed with excitement. "Come, there's something I want to show you."

As he approached her, curiosity piqued, she unveiled an old leather-bound journal – its pages filled with ink-stained maps and half-finished stories. Her eyes sparkled with anticipation as she explained, "I found my old journal! I thought it would be nice for us to read about our childhood adventures together, so we can remember all that we've gone through and look forward to the adventures yet to come."

"Amelia, this is wonderful," Jackson murmured, his heart swelling with gratitude for the woman who had become not only his partner but his compass through life's storms.

"Promise me, Jackson," Amelia whispered, her eyes searching his, "promise me that we'll keep exploring, keep discovering, together."

"Always, Amelia. Always." He vowed, sealing the promise with a tender kiss that spoke of the love they shared, the courage that bound them, and the hope that illuminated their path forward.

And as the sun set behind the Montgomery Ranch, painting the sky in hues of orange and red, Jackson Turner stood tall, his heart warmed by the lessons he'd learned and the love that held him steady. Together with Amelia by his side, he faced the horizon, knowing that whatever challenges awaited them, they were ready – for adventure, for love, and for the future unfolding before them.

If you enjoyed this book, please take a few moments to write a review of it. Thank you!